THE HEART IS RAW

SEASON ONE

SAWYER PAUL

FOR INFORMATION, CONTACT SAWYER PAUL
SP@SAWYERPAUL.COM.

WWW.SAWYERPAUL.COM
WWW.INTERNATIONALOBJECT.COM

ISBN: 978-0-9784803-9-4

ALL WRITING & DESIGN BY
SAWYER PAUL.

PUBLISHED BY GREDUNZA PRESS IN
TORONTO, ONTARIO, CANADA.

THE HEART IS RAW

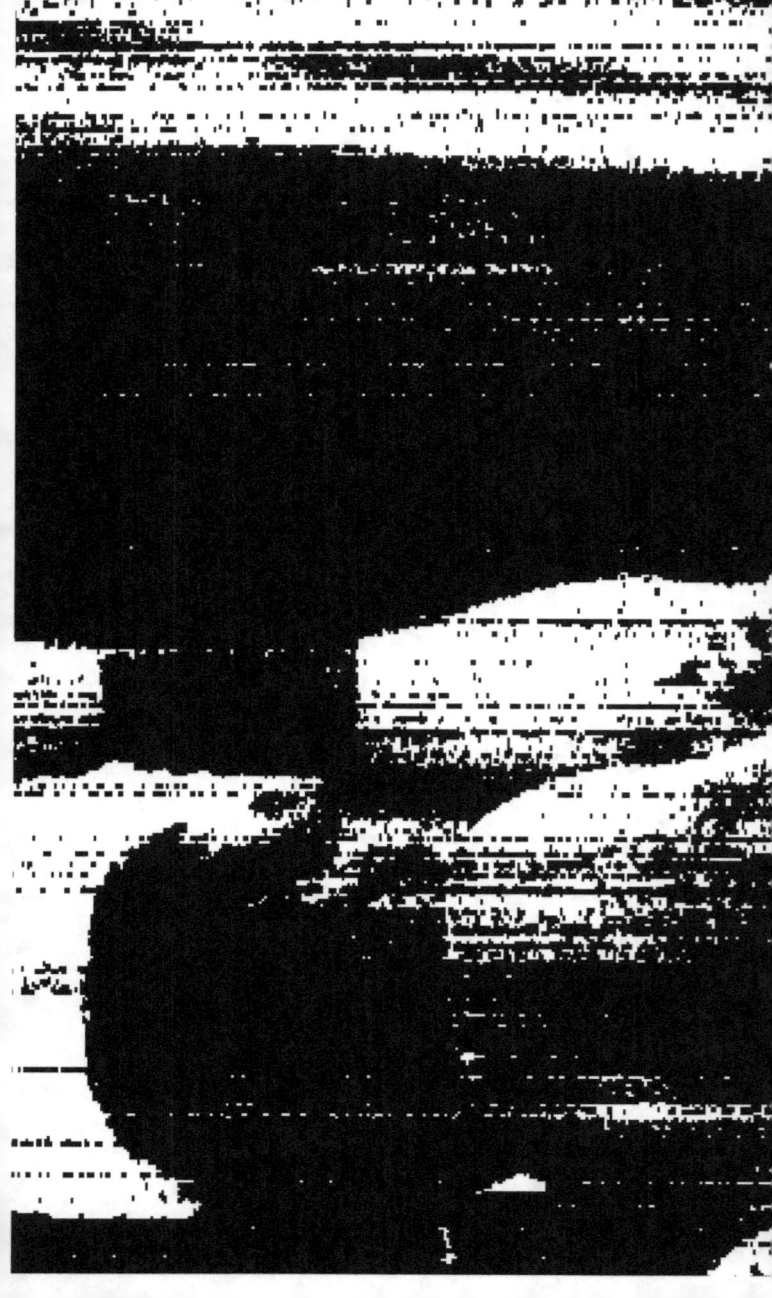

For fake things that still hurt.

THE HEART IS RAW

INTRODUCTION

I used to write about wrestling more often. Over the last year, I've thinned the spigot to the point where my Wrestlemania review was considered a big deal—not because it was good, but because it existed at all. When I began writing about non-wrestling-related topics in IO, it was because I needed to write about other things. I'd lost the thread for wrestling. I didn't know why I was still paying attention.

Something I've noticed is that wrestling is a cipher. It is an open-ended question, one that can only be answered by the viewer. Mick Foley has called wrestling a grand three-ring circus, meaning there's something for everyone (and that there's undoubtedly stuff you won't like), but most wrestling criticism is not only episodic but segmented. It's tough not to do it this way because the show is segmented. Damien Sandow appears on this part of the show. John Cena appears on that part of the show. Fragmentation is inevitable and it's difficult to view the show as a whole. But Raw has never aired as anything other than a full show, so why do we never treat it like one?

What if we view Raw as a cohesive, structured, and purposeful narrative? What happens when we look at the program as something they planned to produce, scene-by-scene, moment-by-moment, in order to achieve something greater than the sum of its parts? What's the point of this episode, in relation to not only its characters but the overall narrative momentum? Finally, what do we get for watching a whole episode and not just a single match or monologue? What's the reward for the viewer?

That's obviously going to be different for everyone, but it's been a while since I've tried to tackle this issue and I'd like to again. I don't know how long I'll do it, but from here on there'll be a review for Raw every Tuesday or Wednesday.

Obviously this last part didn't come true, exactly. I wrote 17 Heart is Raw pieces in 2013, mostly from Wrestlemania in April to Summerslam in August. They are presented in this volume because they tell an overarching story of time, pop-culture consumption, and how we're supposed to feel vs how we can't help but.

I hope it helps, even if it hurts first.

—Sawyer Paul

THE CERTAIN FALL

WRESTLEMANIA XXIX

When I was young, too young to remember proper details like time and place, I rejected God. I couldn't have been more than six years old when it happened. A man I don't remember told me that Dinosaurs were a lie; that they didn't exist because the earth wasn't old enough. You don't tell a kid in the eighties who grew up a few miles away from Drumheller that dinosaurs aren't real.

We have faith in things, even if we can't say why. I had more faith in the reality of dinosaurs than God for tangible reasons. I could touch a dinosaur bone. I could listen to men explain exactly how they existed. I could see them in the ground. What was God in comparison? Stories. Just stories.

I was smart when it came to thinking about dinosaurs. I still believe in them. I still don't believe in God. It was a good bet to make as a kid. For a long time, I was sure that organized religion was one of the worst cancers of the world. Part of me still thinks this, but it's connected to something I'm wrestling with right now. It's a theory, and by definition and circumstance it can't be more than that: I think *certainty* is the worst thing in the world.

I was smart about dinosaurs when I was a kid, but boy was I dumb about pro wrestling. The eventual realization that it was staged didn't have a specific moment, but it was around the winter of 1992. I honestly couldn't tell you when it happened. All I know is that I watched Wrestlemania VII believing everything, and by VIII that specific faith was gone. But wrestling was never 'real' to me the way some once believed. I don't think I ever thought it was a sport (if anything, I wondered aloud why sports weren't exciting like wrestling). It just hadn't dawned on me that it was art; that they were essentially putting on a show for the purpose of entertainment.

I look at the kids in the audience today and wonder what they think of all this. When criticizing pro wrestling, it's all too easy to slip into the armchair writer, dictating what you think should have happened. Mostly, you want the show to be better for you, but often the purpose is purportedly selfless: you want the show to be better for everyone. You want more people to watch the show. You want to be able to talk about it with your buddies again, like in the old days. You want it to be like it used to be, or a better version of what you kind of remember. It's so easy to suggest a better route to a brighter future.

I wonder if the kids these days lose their interest in pro wrestling because they go online and find a gaggle of old men complaining about move speed, or who should have won, what the greater good could gain from different results in a fake sport.

I wonder if the magic goes away when they read about the politics, the burials and the dirt. But I also wonder if a moment on the show will break their faith. I don't mean that they'll realize that it's all a stage. WWE goes way far out of its way to make everyone know that they put on a show, and I doubt even brand new fans ever really think that its 'real.' What I mean is the magic of the low drama, the soap, the special bond that comes from following a series of characters for years.

I want to talk about certainty and doubt. I'm going to do this through the lens of Wrestlemania, an event put on by a company whose currency is the battle between these two ideals. Pro wrestling's staged conflicts provide an illuminated arena for this debate.

"America the Beautiful" didn't open Wrestlemania this year. Instead, we were first greeted with a message from New Jersey Governor Chris Christie. A video played reminding us of the damage caused by Hurricane Sandy, an event which they find themselves still reeling. It segued into a mission statement about human survival: "The strongest force of nature is the resilient human spirit. It's a spirit that's alive on every street and every avenue," Christie said. It is fitting that the first words of the show are from a Republican, a man whose certainty about the President's ability to lead was decimated by the same storm.

The very first match was about doubt. The tagline of the six-man match was whether or not Randy Orton and Sheamus could trust The Big Show. Orton was certain he could. But Orton is also a selfish, preening narcissist, and chose the certainty of his own skill above Big Show's trust. In tagging himself in, going for broke against all three members of The Shield, he failed. He could have given in just a little bit, and it could have turned out differently.

The strength of The Shield as characters so far is in doubt itself. Nobody quite knows what they exist to do, and they are the most opaque characters WWE has. Why are clear definitions always preferred in character sketches?

Ryback lifted Mark Henry over his head. He toppled and knocked himself out. Ryback is a big ignoramus, certain of his own momentum and strength, unwilling to accept any logic that isn't chantable. Mark Henry has the layers of a nearly two-decade career, and his face is one who doubts the future, because he knows the past.

We think our faith is broken once and its over, but that's a lie we tell ourselves afterwards. We think the bandage comes off quickly and we're healed. But we weren't. That's not how it happened. We were cut over and over until it was gone. We like to think it was just one agonizing moment, but it was a coarse magazine, one by little one. With every certainty that is nicked by reality, the few we have left get held tighter.

If God exists, the world is horrible. If wrestling is real, there's one more sport and one fewer art form. Obviously these are lower stakes, but the battle is over the same truth: if magic exists, the world is unfair. Dolph Ziggler toyed with our faith, reenacting a heartbreaking moment from last year. Of course it was a kiss. What breaks hearts more? It was a reflection of a villain we love emasculated by another villain we love. The tag team match was the absolute opposite of the main event: cast with deep, three-dimensional characters who played both to and with the crowd, and entirely too short. You couldn't say it was bad, but it wasn't enough of a good thing.

I liked Jericho vs Fandango fine, but the contest was nothing compared to their spectacular entrances. For Fandango, the dancers were stunning and fitting, a real iconic moment that will help cement his young career. Imaging a fresh Goldust getting an entrance like that. It also opened up a few silly questions: who employs these women? Is it Fandango himself? Is it WWE? Are they divas? Nitro girls? What were they doing the other 99% of the show? And who is the main dancer who accompanies him? I want to know more about her. But I also want that yearning for answers to last as long as possible.

Jericho's fireworks were awe-inspiring. I mean that to be heavy: I was actually in awe at the scale. They had fireworks later on in the show, but nothing like that. They befit a true legend, one I believe WWE sees him as, albeit not one they know what to do about. He doesn't fit their mold. He's bigger than WWE, but there isn't a bigger stage. There isn't a higher place.

Diddy's performance was rote, and I only have one thing to say about it: it sounded worse than the live performers last year. I see the appeal of a musical component, but Wrestlemania's acoustics have never benefited live musicians. Last year, they somehow figured out how to finally make pop stars sound like pop stars, but they forgot the lesson here. Muddled vocals, bad reverb, and negligible bass reared their ugly heads again. Living Color experienced the same technical issues, and Punk's entrance suffered. These aren't in any way the things that make or break a 4-hour wrestling show, but they contributed to the overall feeling that they had trouble hitting the high points of the previous year. There was nowhere to go but down.

The Undertaker's undefeated Wrestlemania streak isn't something I really care about, but I see that people do. They care about it as much as all those shiny championship titles that also have no tangible meaning.

A major complaint I've read in many reviews is that it's incredibly foolish to let anyone wrestle after the Undertaker at Wrestlemania, because the crowd's emotional energy is so wrapped up in the streak that there's not much left after he wins. I think there's more to it than that however, because I don't think people come to Wrestlemania to see the Undertaker win. I think they come to see him come closer to losing than ever before, but never actually *lose*. They want to experience a deeper well every time. At this point, there shouldn't be easy victories for the Undertaker, because it deflates so much of the tension of the entire show. This match suffered from predetermined-outcome-syndrome (something you'd think more fake fights would have) though it'll play much better the second time you watch it. I'm not concerned about the quality, but instead the larger idea. What happens if the Undertaker does eventually lose? What happens to the crowd? What happens to WWE? What happens when a mythos is shattered and the walls come crumbling down?

I've never had a faith in God taken away from me, because I've never believed in a God. But you can't help but believe in the streak. It's real. It's tangible. You can actually count it. Does WWE have the ability to handle its destruction with the proper weight? And are they wise enough to leave it be, knowing they probably don't? Are they certain they can handle that responsibility?

Certainty is the worst even when you're right. Who among you who was certain of Undertaker's victory felt satisfied in winning the gambit? Certainty in the abilities of others is one thing, but certainty in one's own ability is often worse than that. HHH and Brock Lesnar are the two men in wrestling most certain of their status. HHH is certain of his position. He's certain of his talent. He's certain that the crowd cheers for him. He's so certain of all those things that he put his career on the line, certain that people would care.

Career-ending matches are often worse than hair vs hair matches. At least with the latter, someone gets a haircut. About four career-ending matches have actually stuck, making the proposition pretty loose. HHH was certain people would want to see himself vs Brock again, but I'm not sure anyone did. The show would have benefited enormously by giving them both different dance partners. Neither character is really on the show enough, so maybe there were no stakes otherwise. But who knows? Maybe people cared and we couldn't hear them. We couldn't hear the crowd all night. Their vocals went up into the cold, cloudy night and vanished. All we got were faint echoes and lost moments.

There were only two times I was certain what the crowd communicated. The first was the celebration of "Yes! Yes! Yes!" for Daniel Bryan. The second was when John Cena emerged. The people boo'd him. They boo'd him to smithereens.

But before Cena's music played, they announced the attendance, an utterly boggling 80,676. Considering that WWE basically made up the number in 1987, one could argue this was the highest-attended Wrestlemania yet. But then, if you don't know if the number was true in 87, how do we know if this one is? It's astonishing to me what some people feel certain about.

Okay, lets get back to Cena, a man many (including myself) pegged as ready to finally become a villain on this show. That he did not shows WWE's faith in Cena as masthead. Hardcore wrestling fans have never taken to him, and have been calling for his head for the better part of his career. Both Cena and WWE are wholly comfortable with the dichotomy, and they believe there's more to do with Cena as he stands. They don't need to "turn" him for his character to grow. Not everyone needs to become a villain in order to show growth. And why does he need to grow, anyway? Because you're older? How much did you grow this year? Give him a break. The more certain we are about what "needs" to be done with John Cena, the more WWE plants its heels and stays put. Maybe they are listening to you, but maybe they'd like you hit you with a Cubito Aequet. It's tough to say.

John Cena is that guy you hate at work, the guy you concentrate on the way home, and who you complain about to your wife. Maybe he makes a little more than you and you don't know why. Maybe he's the boss's son. You're so sure that this bastard is out to wreck your life, and you hate him for real reasons, but that doesn't make you right—it makes you small. Do you know what it feels like to get over that feeling? Fucking *wonderful*. Try it out. Don't become a blissful hippy douchebag about it, because those people are the *actual* worst (because they're so certain of their own goddamn inner peace), but let go just a little.

Last year's Wrestlemania was headlined by the same match: Rock vs Cena. This year, it was for the WWE Championship, but the macguffin wasn't a title belt but certainty itself. The Rock, a few weeks before the event, laid this idea out. He faced his opponent, John Cena, and proclaimed, "You think you can beat me. I *know* I can beat you." That line telegraphed not only the outcome of the match but the whole event. The certain were wrong. The certain fell. As Rock and Cena stood together in the ring post-match, you could read Rock's lips. He said: "I came back for this very moment." It made me look back on the last two years, a period we can think of as Rock's epilogue. He came back to surprise and delight, then to dominate, and finally to lose. It was as if it was all telegraphed.

It was as if they knew all along it would end this way. I'm sure they knew it. I'm sure this was the plan. I'm sure they were certain this would work.

I chose to go watch Wrestlemania alone instead of watching the premiere of Madmen with my fiancée. It was a week after my thirtieth birthday. I made the wrong decision. I should have watched the show on my own, later. I didn't need to experience this in a communal space, because I don't get any sense of brotherhood from wrestling fans. I should have stayed home and cuddled next to my girl and drank wine and watched Don Draper. I don't say that because I didn't enjoy the show. It's not because I didn't get what I wanted. I didn't go in wanting anything. I bought my ticket because wrestling was something I believed in for a very long time. It's because wrestling is in a place that can't help me right now.

I've used wrestling as therapy for many years, but it's something that has ultimately held me back from personal and professional growth, and I made that choice because of how its presence in my life made me feel. It hasn't made me feel that way in a while, and I need a different relationship from wrestling now. I need different things from my pastimes, but I want wrestling to find me when it can deliver them. If Wrestlemania 29 is any indication, WWE is on its way, but it has a while to go. It hasn't become that thing I need yet, and I'm not certain that it ever will. But I have faith.

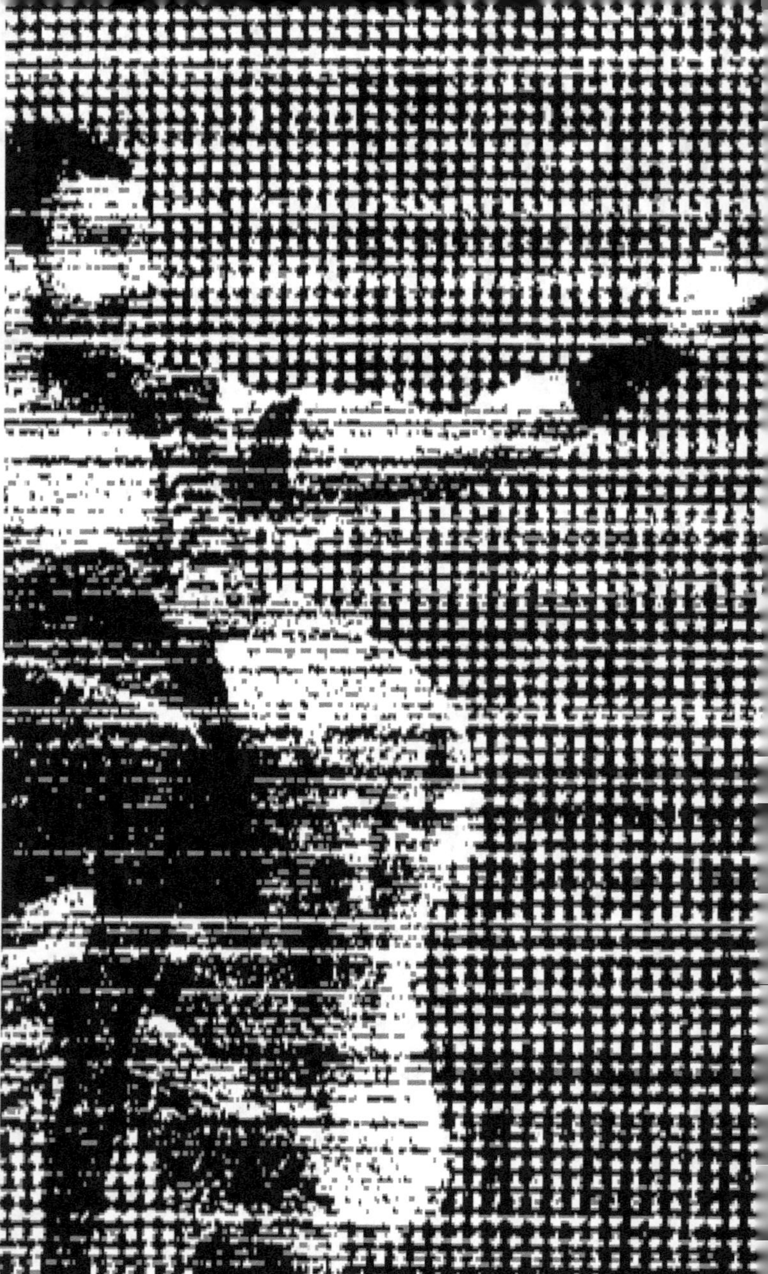

DON'T LET US GET HURT

APRIL 29

What happens to us when we're hurt? Think of the last time your body felt unexpected pain. Your back went out. Your wrist cramped up. Your head pounded. Maybe you broke an arm or pulled a muscle. The first moment is often confusion: what happened here? Things aren't right. For a brief moment, that's all your dumb disorientated nervous system allows. Next comes realization, cold shingles of truth. I've been hurt. I've been knocked down. The facts are all there, but only after clarity comes the pain. You only feel the pain because you've accepted it the reality of the situation.

Then come choices. Do you tell people? Do you hide it? Do you make it seem like no big deal? Do you exaggerate? How you communicate pain is not necessarily about how much it hurts, but how much you want the world to know it hurts. Pro wrestling deals with how to project pain all the time, and the audience gets to answer these two questions every few minutes: How much did it hurt, and how much did it really hurt?

Projected pain is the theme for Raw this week. We know John Cena is in pain. We know this because WWE.com told us. Whether you look at that article as factual reportage or a hype paragraph to watch the show says a lot about how you feel about John Cena's taped ankle.

There are wrestling fans who want Cena in pain, of course. That article made them happy. For a few days, they could fantasize and contemplate the future without Cena. Maybe he'd be off the show for weeks, they thought. Maybe we could have a respite. Maybe he could spend that time granting wishes for sick children. But then, all the kids Cena inspires aren't happy to hear that he's hurt. Maybe they didn't know he could be hurt. The last time he was injured, he was still on every show. He barely missed a beat. And before last fall, can anyone remember when Cena was out for more than a week? It's been *years*. It was before this era. A great number of the kids in the audience don't have a conscious memory of 2007.

The *A* story of Raw this week hinged on this question. If you believed the story, you could feel for John, or you could take pleasure in his obvious discomfort. If you didn't believe it, you could be impressed by his performance. He showed the pain well. He didn't last long. The Shield have defeated eight men in different combinations of health, but a man with one leg is a man with his back to the floor. A new viewer with no knowledge of the strange rules of pro wrestling could put that together.

But Cena's real scene happened earlier, when he walked out with three children from the Make a Wish Foundation.

Raw sometimes acts like a keynote presentation about the company as a whole (often moreso than their quarterly shareholder meetings), and this was WWE showing us the best thing they do. Sure, the show is violent and off-putting, crass and often moronic. But it also makes children really, really happy, and just in case you forgot that, here's a bunch of them. In case anyone forgot why John Cena hasn't become a bad guy yet, look no farther than the forced smiles on those nervous young faces. Notice Cena didn't look in pain here. He couldn't. Not in front of the kids, Mean Gene. Not in front of the kids.

As dominant as The Shield have been, it hasn't been through strongarming, but endurance. The trio haven't been in a match yet where they haven't suffered. Rollins has taken the majority of the impressive tumbles, but Ambrose has received the most clobbering blows. He's been wrapped up in the majority of surfboards and headlocks. He's the one who's had his shirt ripped off, then pummeled by giant fists. Ambrose has showcased incredible offensive zeal, but his talent is in his projected emotions.

He gets beat up better than anyone. Underneath his greasy hair, beyond his insane tongue, I see it: the true fear of a real actor.

The *B* story of the evening involved Alberto Del Rio, or, rather, Del Rio's employee Ricardo. Professional wrestling matches involving characters who aren't wrestlers are often a delight, because WWE knows to cast them with wrestlers who just don't wrestle that often. Ricardo (the physically unimpressive rookie), Langston (the physically impressive rookie) and Zeb Colter (the physically-and-mentally way-gone veteran) put on the most fun dance of the evening (on a show with a literal dance contest). Ricardo somehow won the day (if a silly character *can* win, WWE will make sure that he does), which gave Del Rio the ability to pick the gimmick for his upcoming championship match.

Del Rio wouldn't announce his decision until later on, which gave the announcers a good hour and a half to ponder what he might choose. This is a good thing to do on a three-hour show, since it can too often feel like Raw is just one unconnected scene after another. Del

Rio fought Antonio Cesaro in a very fun contest, then announced that he would fight Dolph Ziggler and Jack Swagger in a ladder match. It was the only choice for the narrative: both his competitors won Money in the Bank ladder matches and cashed in to win the very belt that's on the line. Come to think of it, so did Del Rio. Has anyone on the roster not done so at this point?

For a show that's been on the air for 20 years, one has to accept a little repetition. We saw Sheamus and Mark Henry break apart the scenery not two years ago. We watched Khali win a dance contest and then get attacked like, last year (wasn't it against Jericho? Did I dream that?) We watched Dolph Ziggler defeat Kofi Kingston 400 times. But circumstances have evolved. Ziggler has a bigger championship now. Kofi has a smaller one (it's the same one, but fewer people care). Khali has a girlfriend now, because we're not allowed to watch Natalya wrestle for some reason. Things move forward, even if we are still working with the same people, even if it hurts to see them grow so slowly.

SLEEP, VILLAIN

MAY 6

I watched an old <u>Dylan Moran special</u> on Friday night. It was late and I fell asleep, and I haven't watched it again, so I might get this quote wrong. He began his set by complaining about the length of the day. He said (and I probably misquote): "24 hours is just long enough to get regret, and then you have to go to sleep."

That's the problem with reviewing television programs, or life, or anything, really. A nice thing happens, and then you ground it into dust trying to extract more meaning. Some things are just nice, and should maybe be left alone. This is why good news keeps. This is why nobody is really interested in reading critical theory that concludes with "Well, that was fun."

Antonio Cesaro is the wrestler to watch these days. He's got both trading card and real characteristics. He speaks more languages than anyone not working at the UN. He is a physical specimen, but one built a hundred years ago, with real things from this planet. He looks old but you'll never guess his real age. He's stronger than everyone, including the other guys on the show who are also that. He's the most interesting man in the world. He is superior, and therefore a villain, one we have to watch lose over and over because that's what villains do on episodic television. We're frustrated by that, not because we want to relate to him and be his buddy, but because this is a wrestling show and we are wrestling fans and he's the best guy doing that thing.

There's nothing wrong with that role. Rick Rude played it his whole career. And there's not much evidence to suggest Cesaro is destined for the same platitude; let me point you to CM Punk or Edge's first years with the company to show how things can quickly things can go from treading to greatness. We've graded Cesaro harshly. He's coming out of his first full year. Where was HHH in 97? Kane in 99? Punk in 07? Compare, contrast, and relax.

I'm leading this week with Cesaro because he's a bit player on a show that seems charged to make everyone look like a tiny, fragmented piece. Who is the star of Raw? John Cena? Brock Lesnar? Brad Maddox? It's never clear. There's always just these people who show up, and we think they work there but who knows, really. Thinking too hard about it leads to a simple answer: There is no answer.

You have a guy on the show who wears a thing that gets him called the World Heavyweight Champion, and he's easily the tenth-most important person. You have a General Manager who isn't in charge. HHH is the COO but that's just another title, like the US Championship but not as difficult to get through airport security. When Brock Lesnar destroyed HHH's office, he held tightly to a version of the World Heavyweight Championship. That belt seemed to carry more weight than the one actually in play.

The big victim this episode was HHH's office, [torn apart by Lesnar](). They want you to imagine your own office like this, strewn and shaken by your enemies. They want you to hate this guy, or to want to be this guy. [Who hasn't wanted to take apart some asshole's office]()? That's the point of catharsis only an adult can understand. That desk had it coming.

But let's return to Cesaro. He quickly and easily dispatches the ghost of Zack Ryder, then suggests he has no competition. It's brash, but also idiotic. We've watched him get beaten by everyone in the last four months. He's been around long enough that we want him to be more, but he isn't, at least not yet. He's still just a character.

I'm still impressed that Daniel Bryan and Kane can be in several stories at once. They're fighting the Shield, but they also have a personal vendetta against Ryback. The Undertaker is lurking in their proximity (and will stay there for a while). They're not friends with Cena, but tend to get in his business more than could be called a coincidence. Good guy champions do have a habit of hanging out, so who knows. Maybe there's a clubhouse.

WWE knows that WCW overused the nWo ending far too often, so they're careful about how to close the show with a faction. Ryback defeats Kane in a solid hoss fight Holzerman surely appreciated, then the Shield's music hits. Ryback is the villain of the month, but the Shield are the villains of the year, and the hierarchy is clear. Ryback may have had the last word, but he scrambled for a weapon when the bigger bad guys showed up. John Cena is above Daniel Bryan, but his heroism puts him on the same level. There actually isn't honour among thieves here, and it's refreshing to no end to see that all the bad guys aren't in a cabal.

It's nice to not have to think too hard about where someone stands, even if that person is a bastard or a monster. Critics of pro wrestling will laugh at this. Of *course* it's about white hats and black hats, and that simplicity is antiquated. I'm not championing that the good guys are acting like good guys. I've called John

Cena a hero for the past two weeks, but those are the only two weeks this year he's earned that title. What I'm happy to see is that these characters say what they mean, do what they say, and have characters rise and fall through the cracks in their amour.

As fans, it's tough not to watch the show, think just a little hard about what you didn't like, and then go to sleep. My advice this week is to just go to sleep, and then say what you mean in the morning. I'm very bad at taking my own advice.

UNCERTAIN TITLES

I've had a very uncertain week, professionally and personally. I became frustrated, and when that happens I tend to isolate myself. If I've appeared aloof this week, my apologies. It's been a tough one. For obvious reasons, I can't divulge too many things on a public blog, but you can probably guess. There are only a few things anyone can be really personally upset about. I'm aghast about international relations, but that's something everyone is all the time on some level. My cuts are closer. My rough week has been about me.

I don't know what Dean Ambrose's deal is. I don't know what the Shield's deal is. I have no idea what they want. One episode, they're standing over Kane. They hold his title and pose, as if to say that soon these things will belong to them. Then they do the same thing to Kofi Kingston. Then they attack other people, who have either no belts or bigger belts. Do they care about titles? Do they want them? Is that the point of the group? It can't be something that attainable, right? I mean, the tag team and US titles? Really? Those things? Who wants those?

The Shield is *the* A story of Raw lately, as they overshadow almost every other scene (and in fact, interfere in almost every scene). And if the Shield are the story, Dean Ambrose is the character. That's not to take anything away from Roman Reigns or Seth Rollins, but Dean is the first character to do something other than be a guy in a menacing group. He's the first guy to get a string of singles matches.

He's the first guy to get a <u>sympathetic black and white photo essay</u> (where I got the image above, before I edited it). WWE is an expression-based art form, and Ambrose has one of the most expressive faces since William Regal. I want to watch him perform for hours, but I have no clue what he wants.

That the Sheild's undefeated streak now contains an asterisk only dilutes it. Perhaps the disqualification here is to show that titles might not be so bad.

That's true of a lot of Raw performers, though. Ziggler's in a class by himself for expression, because his whole body is his face, and the removal of his person from the show hung over this whole episode. We take Ziggler for granted. WWE certainly did. And now that he's finally attained a World Championship, he may have also attained something even more valuable: a hearts-grow-fonder moment of leave. Langston is an interesting avatar, since he's nothing like Ziggler in literally any way. It makes us miss him more.

It's excruciating watching people hate their job. It's even worse to empathize with them. I empathize with Lesnar. It's like he's back at the job he had in high school, except now he has a master's degree. The economy sucks, and he chose a narrow field. Maybe he was the best short order cook in the waffle house, but he never, ever wanted to do that. I've always got the feeling with Lesnar hated pro wrestling. He's never looked more bored in all his life. And even if he did, what kind of material have they given him? HHH can be a great opponent, but they sink each other.

Some weeks, the punches hurt even if they don't hit you. I'm sure that's true of these performers, who can hit every kick to the head and land every octopus, and still walk away feeling heavier and tired. That's how I feel this week. That's definitely how Dean Ambrose felt, and the whole damn cast fell in the same way. Some weeks, everyone is working at half speed, and you never fully know why. Sometimes it's the altitude. Sometimes it's the road.

But once in a while we feel beaten because we look up and back at our younger and more vulnerable selves and wonder how we got here, dancing in place, hoping for different results, desperately applying wrist-locks and checking our wristwatches to see if the future we've paid for has arrived, knowing it hasn't, and feeling like it won't.

TIRED, DEAD EYES

MAY 20

So it's warm. You're at a bar, one of those great bars where you can sit at the entrance and drink beer with your partner, and watch the street, spending an afternoon commentating on the world, eating nachos, and generally wading through the day, stress-free. Your phone is in your pocket, and you have no desire to check it for anything; no part of you requires nervous distraction. In a few hours you'll go home, make dinner together, clean up together, and watch a really old TV show, something that aired before your mother was born.

Two interactions with strangers happen before you leave the bar. The first, a thin man with tattoo's and cigarettes and a rolled-up movie poster of the Godfather sits down at the same bench. He says aloud—you assume, to you—"you got a problem?" You haven't looked at this person. You haven't acknowledged his existence, and he's already looking to pick a fight. You shrug. He laughs. "Thought so," as if to say he's won something with your indifference of a person you still haven't looked at. When you hear him interact with the server, you take a quick look. He's smaller than you are, wiry. He's also belligerent to the server, asking for his pint with lazy expletives.

You hear him talking to himself. He's on his cell phone. He talks about this big house he's going to, how he needs to get ready. He talks about wanting to get into a fight tonight. In a few moments, he slams his fist on the bar. You get the feeling that at any moment, you could be in a situation you don't want to be in, and you begin tooling options. You know that any passive comment will likely be met with aggression. Then, you see the server drop the bill next to him, only a few minutes after he's arrived. This is how bars deal with people they'd like to leave. This is the first step. He pays the bill, and doesn't take the hint. He leaves and comes back, smoking on the patio, engaging everyone in proximity. He keeps sitting back down next to you, and you've locked eyes and you see things going sour. Eventually, you speak to the bartender. He knows what's happening, and your complaint is enough for him to use his thick English brawn to muscle the man outside. You hear the bartender say to him "You're making my customers uncomfortable," and you wonder if he'll look over at you. He doesn't. He leaves, threatening the air. In a moment, he's gone.

In a few moments, another man walks up to the counter where your food and drinks and your partners' cell phone rests. He's gaunt and surly and possibly homeless, and you assume things because he asks for money. You refuse him. He asks again. You tell him to go away, that you're not interested in being solicited, and that you'd like him to leave right away. You take care of this yourself. You feel tough for some reason. He tells you to go fuck yourself, but after a moment he's gone, too.

I'm telling this to you because I'm Canadian, and a few weeks ago Rich Thomas, my podcast co-host, asked me if we have the same class-based system that the English struggle with, or if we are more like the American system, where wealth trumps heritage. I honestly don't know the answer. As far as I can tell, Canadians don't seem to value either in any real capacity. We are quick to mock our celebrity pool, and I wouldn't know what any of the 118,000 millionaires in Toronto might look like. We mostly leave one another alone. But how I acted to these two men (twist! That second-person prologue was about me—this was a cribbed version of an experience this week) can only be read in a class-based way. With the angry man inside the bar, I took the polite, authority-based approach. I handled the beggar with direct, cold derision, and I did so because one was on my side of the bar, and the other was not.

Canadian politeness is something you've all heard of, and you generally take it to mean that we're**nice**. But that's not really true. Canadians are pretty much just like everyone else. The politeness is two-faced. The truth isn't something we want to talk about, and what happened to me (or to you, to return it to second-person), is to realize that Canadian politeness has its problems. There are class-based shards stuck in there, just waiting to serrate. There are capitalist-based bombs, waiting for you to cut the wrong wire. And you can't help yourself but forget that it's a built-in, factory feature of your own personality, until it comes out raw, and makes you back up and wonder just what the hell you just did.

There's a class structure in WWE, but it's pallid. There aren't really limits on who can fight who, at least not the type you'd normally associate. There is no weight limit in WWE, and the gender limit is purely contextual. There are no brackets or qualifications, as much as most wrestling websites would like to think these exist. But, if you watch the show for a long time, you come to realize that there are quiet, polite systems at play that keep characters from one another. John Cena and Kofi Kingston almost never appear together, for instance. You could say that it's because they aren't fighting one another, or that they aren't on-screen friends (though, really, nobody is on-screen friends with Cena anymore). But it really has everything to do with the fact that Kofi isn't in Cena's league. Cena only interacts with characters who have made it to his level, or people WWE would like to reach it. Kofi is situated at a certain station, incapable of moving forward without strapping some kind of metaphorical rocket to his back. Maybe he should kick someone through a window.

Daniel Bryan has lost to the Shield every time they've been in the ring together. When it's two on three, or three on three, they've never pinned his partner. Okay, they pinned Cena that one time, but they mostly just pin Bryan. This time they pinned Kane, but it doesn't matter. Bryan got all the taunting. We forget that this is only Bryan's fourth year in WWE, because he's changed so much since NXT Season 1. He's no longer the indie veteran hoping to prove himself in the big leagues. He's not even his second character, the delusional world champion who used the DENNIS system on AJ Lee. He's this third thing, and he's perhaps about to become a fourth. Maybe this new version will be the one to propel him past his current class, that fat roster of former World Champions with years left on their career.

It's tough to see these lines as fans, but it's even more difficult to break through them as performers. What the hell are you supposed to do? Change your name? Change it again? Try out half a dozen different character types? Pretend Kofi Kingston is a "pro" compared to you? Disappear for years, only to return out of nowhere? Surely, some part of this had to set sparks. Did it, Curtis? Did it, Michael? Did it, Joe?

The "Curtis" in "Curtis Axel" is great. The "Axel" is not, because it's supposed to be referencing an axe but it makes me think of a tool. It's not a good idea to make me think of tools when looking at fresh pro wrestlers. Hey, why not just go with "Curtis Hennig"? The intro was solid, but nothing compared to Lesnar's original introduction. But of course this isn't an introduction. We know who this guy is. We've seen him flounder. This is a repackaging, and a pitch, where the interesting angle is not the product itself but what it's up against. Axel's first opponent is HHH. That's a different class.

The character of "Curtis Axel," is simply Michael McGillicutty with added Paul Heyman. Heyman has made a career as a kingmaker, but his secret is seeing greatness and pushing for it. Heyman has never done much with guys of meagre charisma. The idea here is that Joe Perfect *is* phenomenal, but only Heyman can really see it right now. If you look into his tired, dead eyes, do you see anything? I guess we're supposed to have faith that Heyman does.

I'd like to think I see the best in people, but I can't help but give into context. I once had to listen to a man berate a cashier at a Kinko's, accusing her of treating him poorly because he wasn't wearing a suit. I interjected, telling the man that he's being treated like everyone else, and she was doing her best with his irrational requests (he was asking for items Kinko's would never sell). He was insane, so it didn't end rationally. I don't know if they appreciated me chiming in. I never know when that's the right thing to do. I have too many life choices where I could go either way on charm or aggression, and it's never clear which way is right. Do you do what's polite? Or do you do what you feel is right? Well, do you, cowboy?

You're not supposed to solve problems with aggression, because sometimes you wear yourself out more than your opponent. You think you're winning, but then you're on the floor, gassed out, old, out of touch, distrusting the help around you. But what choice do you have? The last guy you tried to reason with broke your arm.

PINK GLASSES

MAY 27

I was 9 years old when Bret Hart won his first WWE Championship. Everything about it felt different, from the place he won it (in Saskatchewan, and on television, instead of in a big arena on PPV) to how people heard about it (anywhere from a week to several months later). It was super weird that he won it at all, since his character had been largely the same since he became a singles wrestler two years prior. Usually something has to happen to you in wrestling to get a promotion, but with Bret, wrestling changed. The steroid trial and major exodus of talent left them with few options. But that's the thing with Bret: his character stayed consistent with his desires, goals, and limitations. It made him incredibly polarizing.

I've always argued that Bret was one of the strongest character in wrestling for this reason: his character lived by a set of principles, and his stories were about those principles crashing up against heavy walls. I feel like that should be *every* wrestling character. Good, bad, or somewhere in the spectrum, characters should believe in something, and stick to those beliefs even if it means their downfall (*especially* if it means their downfall, because that's often the best ingredient for drama). Even villains should stick to their principles, because those beliefs may come into vogue, and that sort of commitment can create an organic anti-hero (see Austin, Steve). That's why I think that bad guy characters shouldn't be evil so much as coarse. The good guys shouldn't be *good* so much as somewhat easy to like. This has everything to do with relentlessly reading the zeitgeist.

WWE decided to make tonight's Raw a Bret Hart appreciation night. They would air the majority of it on the app, something I can't participate in because I have a Windows Phone and WWE hasn't made an app for the platform yet. I'm sure it was nice. He only appeared on the show proper a few times, mostly to give advice and to repeat advice.

You can say what you like about Cena and Ryback—and god knows, there's lots to say. But the main event stipulation for Payback—a three-stages-of-hell with the three worst gimmick matches ever— That's character consistency to the fullest. The lumberjack match doesn't make sense because nobody on the WWE roster likes either guy. The tables match doesn't make sense because neither Cena or Ryback are any good with tables. The only thing that makes sense is the ambulance match, because ambulances are Ryback's gimmick. He didn't have one before, and now he does. The ambulance is what separates him from Goldberg. Losing in matches with lame stipulations is what separates John Cena from Hulk Hogan.

People who like John Cena and Ryback will probably like this match. People who don't like them probably won't, and now nobody else has to wrestle these kind of matches on the show. All the stuff you may not like about WWE is concentrated in a 20 minute portion at the end. Look, they've done the hard work for you.

Character consistency often flies in the face of obvious rivals, since wrestling often hinges on the good guy vs bad guy paradigm so heavily, so it's almost always refreshing to see two bad guys fight. Wade Barrett is solid and dull; Fandango is all flash, so it makes perfect sense that they wouldn't like one another. The fact that they're both villains was ignored, and the match was better for it.

Finally, we come to Chris Jericho's interview with Paul Heyman, which gave us a nice history lesson. You might think this was a case of character consistency being thrown out the window ("You don't get to sit at home and call yourself the best in the world," says the guy who does that all the time), but I thought it was clever. The last time Punk and Jericho fought (about a year ago), they were in different places. Jericho was a dick, and Punk was trying to play nice. Now, Jericho's playing nice (still a dick), and Punk is taking a break, something Jericho has established as something one should do from time to time.

This was Jericho's "I still remember Summerslam. I owe you one," moment. Time moves forward. Circumstances change. But Jericho the good guy is just Jericho with a laugh track. I expect Payback will be when that gets set right. This match is happening so Punk can return cheered, but also so they can put The Best in The World At What He Does back in proper alignment.

One of Bret's greatest criticisms in his career was that he took everything too seriously. Wrestling is a ridiculous thing, and Bret set himself aside all that (the subtitle of his book spelled that out quite obviously). He accepted that wrestling was a cartoon, but that he was a real thing. This quality can breed contempt among one's contemporaries, and also one's fans, who might prefer to see you differently than you might see yourself. This has undoubtedly happened to Bret, a guy painted as someone who didn't "get it" when the tide shifted.

I've received the same criticism with my writing over the years, because I try to take this cartoon world of pro wrestling pretty seriously. I get that it's overblown silliness, but I still think there's a core of real art here, and that the art should be unpacked. The meaning of pro wrestling doesn't lie with who goes over, who gets a push, or any other vulgar anachronism from the 30's.

The art is communicated in the matches and interactions, in the long con somewhere between thirty minutes and thirty years. The beauty of it emerges when you see these fake fighting moves communicate something larger. It's what that larger thing is that makes the principle—and we fight not for flesh and blood, but for principalities. Bret Hart taught me that.

RERUNS

JUNE 3

How's that old cliché go? There's always someone being born who hasn't seen the Flintstones? That one has legs, and I find all sorts of occasions for it. It's a wildcard reasoning for presenting the same thing over and over, even if the majority of people watching have already watched it. The reason content creators get away with repeated material is that they feel there's either a new audience waiting for entertainment, or the same audience not minding watching again. Wrestling may not have reruns, but it does recycle. It does reuse. Like any good soap, the same elements crop up over and over, often dealt with by the same characters in the exact same way. You're watching a repeat even if you don't realize it.

That's how I felt this week. I watched television, went to work, and spent time with the same people I usually spend time with. It's not a revelation or even a novel insight to suggest that some weeks are going to seem more mundane than others, but it got to me a little. I understand that not every experience is going to widen my understanding of the universe, but that doesn't mean I'm not allowed to be a little dulled by a long string of ordinary. So long as I can trudge up the effort to dig up, stupid, I should be just fine.

How far back do you think WWE wants you to remember? The message is mixed. They love to warm your sense of nostalgia, because the show is filled with callbacks and references to previous stories, characters, and situations. But at the same time, they'd perhaps like you to forget just how recently they've presented this exact set of circumstances. I think they'd like you to remember the chess set, but not necessarily the movements of the pieces.

Of course, you may look at Miz vs Barrett as a repeat ad infinitum, and you wouldn't be wrong. The addition of Fandango to the mix makes that story even more of that thing you probably don't want. Sheamus and Cody Rhodes have certainly had that exact match before, with the same ending. How would it end any other way? With plot progression? Come on, what midcard do you think you're watching? And what's this? Daniel Bryan laying flat near the end of the show while the "real" stars stand and stare at one another?

And yes, things are different now. Of course they are. Say what you will about John Cena, but he *is* the evolution of Hulk Hogan and Steve Austin. He has Hogan's unshakable political power without the sliminess, and he has Austin's grit without the mature rating. He plays the game better than anyone, so much so that a large majority of the viewers turned on him early and never wavered. I wonder how much of that derision is personal or whether they just don't want a Hogan-type good guy as the main character. But because he's the same class of character, we unfortunately get the same class of story. Villains of the week, determination winning the day, and an utter lack of hubris, even as he gets hit by a hundred chair shots.

But there are some fun details that are new. Of all people, Khali is getting mileage out of Fandango. He's 2-0 against the guy, if you count dance-offs and cowardly exits as victories (and it's pro wrestling, so why don't we?) AJ Lee is 10% unhappier about her rookie pick losing whenever she doesn't directly interfere. And while the main event was an exact repeat of last week, at least the performers were awake this time. Axel finally showed some skip in his step, mostly while being flung around (remember, *falling* is just as much a wrestling move as anything else).

But then something new happened. Axel had a steel chair, but didn't immediately attack Cena. Instead, he sized him up, and the two had a pretty cool moment I'd never seen before. Axel winds up and runs at Cena, and Cena ducks. Axel tries again: Cena ducks, and dropkicks the chair into Axel. This description doesn't give credit to how long they took to do this. It wasn't a magnificent display of athleticism, but of *timing*, which is the one thing WWE rookies usually lack. New guys always rush through everything, and Axel does, too. But that was a nice moment that showed promise, and moments of promise is all we can ask of the schlub right now.

Sometimes you can do something new just by reversing the order. The Usos and the Prime Time Players have fought a million times, but the Usos rarely win. That they won—and won so dominantly—means they want you to think something has changed. Maybe something has. Sometimes that's enough to keep moving forward.

But then you see HHH argue with Stephanie and Vince, and you're immediately transported back nearly fourteen years, not to when things were better, but at least when it was the first time (not *the* first time, of course. But perhaps *your* first time) you dealt with this crazy family. You know it's not over. You know it'll never be over. It's going to happen over and over, not because it's the best thing going today, but because nobody is tracking your knowledge. You show up, and WWE has no idea what you know. They can't assume you know anything. They aren't afforded the luxury of history. All they know is you're here, so they do what they can. They do what they know. And if some weeks seem more like reruns than others, it's because we've all been here a really long time.

WHO IS YOUR CURTIS AXEL?

JUNE 10

Who is your Curtis Axel? Or rather, *what* is your Curtis Axel?

You're a big deal. You have grown, and leveled up, and you fight bigger battles than you used to. You move on because bigger challenges await. But it doesn't matter who you are; sometimes you fail the test. Someone or something that should be beneath you finds its way under your skin. You used to handle these problems all the time, and you enjoy the fighting nostalgia of an old kind of conflict. But you are above it. You are beyond it. So why are you acting this way?

Don Draper has lots of Curtis Axel's. Sometimes its a client, sometimes a mistress—and for one episode, Ginsberg—but he's no different from us. He is a pillar of male fantasy, but even he succumbs to keyhole fantasies of past conquest. So why are we loath to see HHH experience as the same thing? Was HHH flailing in the ring, attempting to fight Axel over and over as Vince stopped him, any different than Don searching for an ad in the archives that will convince his mistress to return?

But we'll get to that.

I love the little WWE app animation. I really do. If you haven't seen it, it's a new take on the cut-away. Two wrestlers are in a match, but WWE wants to relay some visual information either related to the match, or something entirely inconsequential. Usually, they would cut away and show the thing, or they would split the screen and show both scenes. Now, an absolutely nondescript smartphone flies in from the left, spins around to show the screen in landscape, and the supplementary scene plays. There is no sound, other than the commentary team explaining to you what's happening on the tiny screen, the purpose of the tiny screen, and how you can have this experience in your hand with your own tiny screen. They keep saying "you can only get this content with our app" but then they show it anyway, right up on your 200" 4k 3DTV (presumably. I don't know your setup). Sometimes they'll show the supplemental material with some delay, but there is almost nothing "exclusive" to the app.

If there was any media company perfectly at ease with saying one thing and showing another, its WWE. That disconnect is responsible for lots of viewers to think that some things don't make sense. To WWE, that's fine. They're going to do their best to explain some things, but certainly not everything. They're never going to explain why last weeks' intro, where Vince and Stephanie McMahon called us all a bunch of bloodthirsty barbarians. I mean, they wanted us to boo them, right? Vince actually said "Hey, don't boo my daughter," as if there is any audience reaction to that plea other than boo'ing louder. Wrestling fans love being told what to do, but they prefer it in the form of yes/no suggestions where the correct answer is drunkenly yes ("If anyone here would like me to stun anyone in this ring, give me a hell yeah!"). But why boo them? Why now? Well, I think its because they'd like you to cheer for HHH. Hmm, sure, fine. That makes some sense. You'd like to see him fight, and his family is stopping him. But boo'ing that decision rides on you caring about HHH, which is at this point either in the bag or never, ever going in that bag. Maybe they want you to react to Curtis Axel, as if cranking on HHH sympathy we'll react violently towards his green opponent. That's one way to do it I suppose, but for my money I'd just as well have Axel actually contract a verb at some point and *do* something.

Last week, I was fucking morose in stereo. It was an interior sadness, one wrapped in my own issues and no one else's. I began writing a new book two months ago, and I got down on myself about the entire system. I have negligible patience for the book industry (where finished manuscripts are hacked to death and shelved for years before it's 'right' for the season, where margins are thin and the author is powerless), so I'm a self-publisher. I'm more than happy to sell my own wares. But I'm also tired of the novel model (write for two years, talk about it for a month until your social media relationships are strained, repeat). I was thinking of scrapping the book, until a few days ago. Something happened. I found a new model. It's exactly what I needed, and it's perfect and solves all my problems.

My idea of what a book 'should' be, that's my Curtis Axel. It's tough to let something go. I know the feeling. I've had so many Curtis Axel's in my life. After university, it was my obsession with becoming a teacher. After high school, it was being a DJ. After junior high, it was that girl from junior high (and I'm still not over her). Some years it was pro wrestling, but the bastard just won't let me go.

I'm partially concerned that my general happiness is tied to my feelings about fiction writing, but I'm mostly happy that I can fix my general happiness by opening up a new Scrivener document.

It may be hard to see, but the penultimate scene of the show was something new. Yes, the scene was hackneyed, Vince was an out of touch old man, Steph was unnecessarily shrill, and HHH was holding the idiot ball.

But this was a scene on a wrestling show where the conflict began as one guy wanting to fight another guy (fairly common) and concluded with that guy no longer wanting to fight that other guy (which never, ever, ever happens). A wrestler deciding not to fight is unheard of. It's the very essence of the soap. It's like a Maury guest not caring about who the father is. It's like a Days of Our Lives character just being fine with the amnesia. It's like a CSI detective just letting the case go unsolved so he can go home and be with his family. This shit does. Not. Occur.

But there's a first for everything. A pro wrestler was bound to say "Screw it, I actually am above this fight" and mean it. Maybe they'll reverse this next week and actually go through with an ironman match, but I doubt it. I think he's moving forward, to bigger and better.

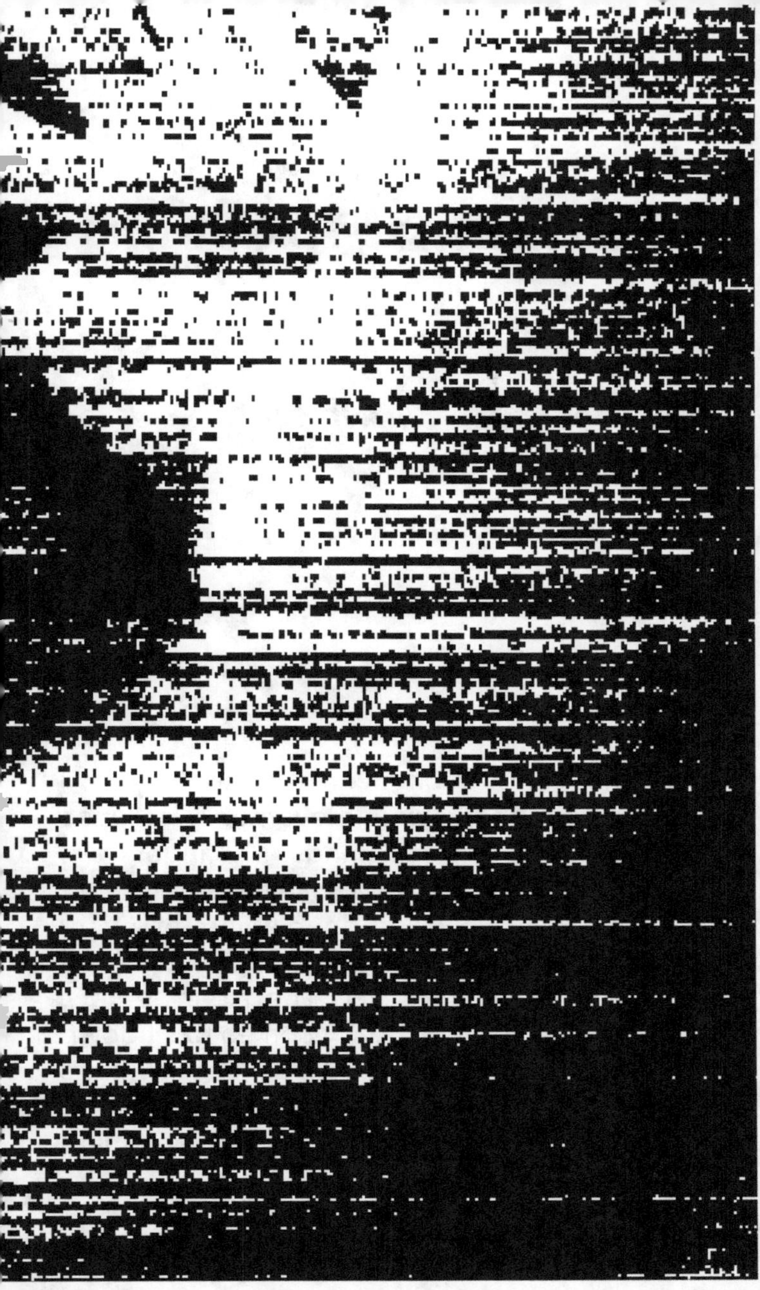

WANTING TO GET UP

JUNE 17

Every time I begin to write an article, I stare at the keys and eventually collapse my head into my hands. My fingers slip through my hair, and I'm left with the work ahead. This is the beginning of every new thing, and while I can't wait all week long to begin writing The Heart is Raw, when the time actually comes to sit down and do the work, I hit The Wall. Writer's block isn't a thing that ever goes away. As you get a little better at overcoming it, it only adapts; it attacks in new ways, and is immediately immune to your old defenses. Yes, writer's block is The Borg, but it's also me, and *only* me. There is nobody kicking me out of this chair. There is no gun to my head stopping me from writing. There is only the fear.

At first, I was afraid that people would hate my writing, but then I published a bunch of things people hated and it didn't kill me, and I got over that one. Then, I became afraid of being ignored, but then I published some stuff I thought was great and nobody read it. Even close friends and family haven't read it. That's fine. I got over it. So if I'm writing the way I like for an audience I like, what's the next fear? Consistency.

Can I keep it going? Will all the stuff I like about my writing just go away one day? I've written just over half a dozen THIR articles and I'm already scared of running out of steam. I haven't yet gotten over this one, and if comic artists are any indication, I likely never will. Consistency is showing up every day with something new. Consistency is knowing that people expect something very specific from you, and deviating at all from what they're used to can destroy all the hard work. The fear of consistency is why comedians go crazy, superhero writers kill their creations, and why nobody cares about professional wrestling, even if it's better than it ever has been.

But consistency is also why so many people tune into pro wrestling. The expectation that this new episode will not only feel familiar but build on acquired knowledge is attractive to both people who think about their TV viewing habits *and* people who have never ever thought about their TV viewing habits. Pro wrestling is addictive for the same reason as the 24-hour news cycle: a sharpened strain of reality, organized into digestible portions, repeated and repeated until your nose bleeds. Neither the news nor pro wrestling has reruns, but the instant replays, and "here's what you missed earlier" bumpers can't help but communicate that they think you want to see the same thing over and over again.

Money in the Bank was special exactly once, but one out of three showings is perfectly decent for a wrestling series. There hasn't been a good Summerslam since 2001, after all, and only one in every five Royal Rumbles are worth it. Payback may never happen again, but if they go with a different name for their experimental June showing, the name will have 100% satisfaction return. I quite liked it, because it appealed to the kind of wrestling fan that I am. WWE focused so much on the losses, on the consequences of hubris—especially with its heroes—that I feel the show speaking to me, and Payback seemed built for my pleasure.

I'm still not entirely sure who the desired audience is for Monday Night Raw. You'd think WWE would want to convert free viewers into paying viewers. But I don't know, man. Sometimes it seems they want you to just sit there and eat hamburgers and be generally dissatisfied. Do we have to use your damn app to enjoy the show? What if we were perfectly happy with the AOL fansite from 1997?

I've always liked Dolph Ziggler enough, but I can't say I've ever felt for him until Payback. Del Rio, a hero, decided he cared about winning the World Title far more than not giving Ziggler more concussions, so that happened. Ziggler's zeal has always been in splaying himself limb as a corpse, the embodiment of everything it is to lose, but for the first time ever I felt the crush of inevitable failure. The world was against him, and he buckled. Some days it doesn't matter how much you *want* to get up.

I'm used to Ziggler falling down, and I like that he's improved at it on an emotional level. It was satisfying but also utterly strange to see Ziggler in the role of the hunter the next night on Raw. If you didn't see it, Ziggler literally chased Del Rio off to the delight of all. This was a man who, as of literally a minute before his match on Sunday, was a reviled villain for the last seven years straight. It wasn't consistent for Ziggler, but it was exactly what anyone else would do in that situation, which is basically the same thing with pro wrestling.

Forever, we got used to seeing CM Punk on Raw as the WWE Champion. Like many others, I became so used to him as champion it became difficult to imagine the show without him. Since Wrestlemania, Punk has been on vacation (well deserved, something more wrestlers should insist) and now that he's back it's just like good old times. In the main event, he shines. He knows how to wrestle slowly without ever dragging, so his matches are easy to follow even in the nosebleeds. It's not clear yet if it's playing a hero or villain this season, but I for one am just glad to get back into the habit of watching him every week.

I'm even more glad to see Christian back, because the show needs more people who look and talk like human beings. That's always been Christian's greatest strength and weakness. If you're just a guy or girl who is looking for someone somewhat relatable in this absurdist universe, Christian is your fella.

I want all these people to keep doing things on this show that I like forever. However, I know that's just not something that can be. As John Cena emphatically stated, he won't get to be WWE Champion forever. We won't have anyone here forever. One day, Ziggler will leave (probably on a stretcher). Cesaro will stop holding up the show's middle hour with excellent technical bouts. And CM Punk will stop sticking the landing in the main event (because being attacked by your next major opponent is also a wrestling move). It won't be consistent forever, as much as they'd like you to think that service hasn't just remained, but improved over time, even if you, the loyal weekly viewer, isn't at all aware of it.

TO LOSE WITH PURPOSE

JUNE 24

I'm listening to the new She & Him album on repeat while writing this, because faux-retro swing pop is one of my favourite crutches. I can get through pretty well anything when someone from this era sings like they're from *that* era. "Who am I without all your affection?" Zooey Daschenel asks a minute in. "I'm a nobody too." I'll get to why that's a wrestling metaphor later, but for now I want the spotlight on me and the other wrestling reviewers. Why the hell do we do this? Why do we tell you what happened on a show you almost definitely watched? I'm not about to look up the data, but I'll take the risk that there isn't a huge audience of "wrestling review" fans out there, and if there are, they're certainly all for Stroud.

I think the compulsion to write about the flagship wrestling show is the attempt to stamp your own palimpsest on the product. We want people to watch the show, and then read our opinion, and slowly cloud their knowledge and flavor of the product with our voice. It isn't about the money; it's the branding. As you read this, you inevitably meld your own thoughts with mine. Sometimes you steal mine. Sometimes I'll read a review and steal an opinion in my mind, so that when I think about that moment on the show I can't separate it from the opinion in the review. For a long time, I thought this was poisonous, and to a degree I still believe that. But it's only poisonous if you would have enjoyed the show without the review, if your opinion changes to the negative after being infiltrated by the opinion of a stranger.

The compulsion makes us do things like add opinions to an otherwise objective reporting of the facts. There are almost no wrestling reviews on any major site without an opinion attached, and the reason is that opinions are more popular and addictive than facts. Facts you can get from WWE.com (most of the time), but opinions are unique (most of the time).

I'm not interested in talking about Raw proper. The show is so formulaic (not a bad thing) that one report inevitably appears like the next. Randy Orton and Daniel Bryan have fought one another for three shows in a row now. I'm writing my reviews this way because I want each and every one to be unique, personal, and painful. Therapy is hard work, and I want this article to be therapeutic. This is selfish, since you might want to read about the show, but I'm here because the show is a device I use to feel better. It's a crutch I want to study. I want to see how it holds me up. Wrestling is the blanket, and this is my journey to figure out why, how, and "really? *This*?"

Wrestlers win and lose matches all the time, but few wins are really victories. Daniel Bryan beat Orton on Smackdown by countout, which in his head means he lost. Last week, the match had to be stopped due to an injury nobody can verify as being real or not, which resulted in a draw, and Bryan thought he lost. He's won dozens of matches since Wrestlemania, but did he, in his head? Is it a victory if it just leads to the same bullies beating you up next week?

Throughout the week, the story we heard from the rumour mill was that tonight was the night Orton was going to finally lose to Bryan, that this was going to propel Bryan to some kind of new level, and that everyone would be happy to see it. Randy Orton is the flipside to Bryan: he's lost many matches in the last few years, but he's never lost a series, or a feud, or any face whatsoever. Mikey Llorin coined Orton's gimmick since early 2011 as "the guy who wins," and it's astonishing just how correct that call has been. Nobody has been talking about Orton here, because he's generally a pretty boring character. But to perform a real loss is rare to Randy, far rarer than a big win for Bryan. That's the story here.

Randy Orton has shown stabs of brilliance in his career, but it's a very rare episode where I'm excited to see him appear. This is partially because his theme music is dreadful, really, the worst music on any show in the history of television, second only to his previous theme, good god that one was bad, so bad I liked his current music for a while simply because it was a respite, but I've learned to hate the new theme nearly as much, a born-again kind of hatred for a piece of art inside a piece of art that slowly eats its host alive. I hate how slow he is, especially because I know he *can* be fast, can cut a pace at a higher degree, can really excite and inspire but regularly chooses to do none of these things.

And I hate the RKO, really the worst move ever, because I was raised as a child partially by Gorilla Monsoon's announcing and move analysis, and he told us all it was a terrible idea to end up in a worse situation than your opponent, to strike in a way that would hurt you just as much, that these moves were rookie mistakes young hotshots attempted before becoming smart and grounded, that no veteran would ever potentially harm himself to finish off an opponent. The RKO ends with Orton's opponent on his front with his arms above Randy Orton, who is on his back, and they are both on the mat, and if the opponent doesn't jump up from the intensity of the impact and bounce around like a cartoon, then the opponent is in a position to *pin* Randy, and he always has been, ever since 2003, for ten straight years, and it's just a dumb variant of the Diamond Cutter anyway, which Page delivered with the desperation of a Jersey everyman and it made so much more sense as Page just sort of slid down, not hurting himself in the process, his opponent folding awkwardly like it might actually hurt or something.

Orton is at his best as an unpredictable psychopath, but for two straight years has played a silent hero, attacked from all angles by increasingly less appetizing villains, without a purpose other than to win, win, win, win, win, until everyone is beaten and nobody is better for it, least of all Orton, who has Cena's problem with empathy but a thousand times worse because he doesn't look like any human being I've ever met or loved.

So to see him lose, to lose with the purpose of finally elevating everyone's favourite pro wrestler to proper main event status, this is a big ticket indeed. WWE is aware of this as Big Deal, and because they like to screw with us (and because we like to be screwed with), they begin the show proper with Bryan and Orton, only to stop the match thirty seconds in due to their outside brawling. "Double disqualification?" Bryan yells at our authority figures, demanding something be done, demanding a *real* match later in the show. Brad Maddox— WWE's resident Bob Benson kiss-ass/ possible serial killer—refutes him, but Vickie Guerrero grants it, if only to make Maddox nervous about being pummeled by Bryan. The viewer is nervous that the match will again be delayed, perhaps to Smackdown, perhaps to the Money in the Bank PPV, perhaps to a string of house shows to be appreciated by the live audience who pay with money but not by us, the loyal TV audience who pay by watching both ads and the app and with hashtags and sarcasm.

But we were rewarded for our attention, given a mammoth main event with a Big Fight Feel, a violent and cathartic street fight involving weapons, in-crowd fighting, and scores of shots with an increasingly broken kendo stick that factored into the wonderful finishing moment. But since winning isn't necessarily a victory, Orton stood after his submission and shook Bryan's hand, finally conceding a respectful loss, making it really count. It reminded me Summerslam 2004, when Orton defeated Benoit for his first World Championship, and Benoit forced Orton to shake his hand and "be a man." Orton has been gaining my affection recently, and I'd like to think this is the beginning of something interesting for both men. But even if it isn't, we have had a satisfying series of events, a well-told beginning, middle, and end, and at the end of the day this happens so rarely in soaps, sports, and everything in between, we should relish and appreciate it—Orton and all.

You've got your match.

MISS WELL

JULY 1

What is a good dropkick?

I know, it sounds like a stupid question. It's like, a dropkick, right? Everyone knows what a dropkick is. Why am I asking this? What a dumb question, right? Okay, well. Let's take this slow. What makes it a wrestling move? What makes a dropkick a wrestling maneuver? Is it that it strikes the opponent and weakens them? If we go by that, then we can suggest that a wrestling move is only a move when it is successful.

But what about a failed dropkick? What is that? Is that an attempt of a wrestling move? What if I add in a small wrinkle to this question and point out that the dropkick was never supposed to hit the opponent? That it was all along supposed to be a failed dropkick, and that missing the dropkick properly—as opposed to hitting it properly, which is an altogether different type of missing, since a proper dropkick doesn't actually connect, but we'll get to that—is in fact the goal?

And that there are varying qualities to a missed dropkick, and one can perform a missed dropkick any number of ways? Dolph Ziggler's missed dropkick is very different from Daniel Bryan's, for instance, and they are both considered hugely athletic and well-balanced. But it is also different from Sheamus' missed dropkick, and of course Cena's. Cena's dropkicks are worthy of study simply because they exist, because a man of his stature should not *be* performing dropkicks, partially because he cannot perform them at the same quality as a Dolph Ziggler, but also because a dropkick communicates something about a performer that perhaps John Cena doesn't need to show, or shouldn't show, or actually maybe *should* show, and we're missing the point because all we see is a heavy man try to fly.

That was a lot in one paragraph, so I'll distill it. Wrestling is scripted and choreographed, and we can be led to believe that a missed maneuver is one done purposefully, and if something is done purposefully in a performance, then it can be done either well or poorly, or anywhere in between, and the parameters of this quality can change based on perspective, all of which is utterly impossible to measure because art is hard.

So my question becomes, is a failed dropkick a good dropkick? It is choreographed and performed, and a failed dropkick performed properly adds to the wrestling match in that it can add drama and heighten tension. A mistake has been made. It offers up the opportunity for an opponent to capitalize. It hurts the performer, but adds to the match itself. Is that a wrestling move? And is a wrestling move anything that progresses the match? Is it anything a wrestler *does*? That's can't be right.

John Cena performed a dropkick on this episode of Monday Night Raw, in his match against Alberto Del Rio. Del Rio launched himself off the top rope, and Cena defended himself by performing a dropkick. He hit it, and Del Rio fell. Cena also fell, because a wrestler who performs a dropkick usually falls. To the viewer, the dropkick appeared awkward, ill-timed, and to no real benefit for Cena. He looked just as hurt as Del Rio. What was the point? To buy time with something unexpected, right? To throw your opponent off guard so you can recover, of course. If we go with that, I can suggest that dropkicks are about time at a cost. Dropkicks are about time. Wrestling moves are about time. How many wrestling moves constitute a good match? Can a wrestling match be one move long? If you like fingerpokes then yes! Otherwise it gets thorny. These are bigger questions that I'll get to some other time, but I wanted to put a pin in them here.

People who don't watch wrestling probably don't know this, but a dropkick is almost always a defensive maneuver. You can't really dropkick *at* someone and have it make sense, unless you have incredible propulsion and momentum on your side (tall, skinny fellows do well here). It generally only works when the opponent is running towards the performer in a way in which they can't stop; their force pushing forward at such a rate there would be no way they could simply stop in their tracks, forcing the performer of the dropkick to simply jump in the air and promptly land on their face. The counter to the dropkick is to *stop*. Wrestlers do this by grabbing the rope and holding on, reeling from their own momentum, watching with desperate glee when their opponent leaps for a dropkick and finds empty air, falling and hurting themselves in a way they would somehow not if the move had landed, even though the performers' body goes through exactly the same motion either way. Is that a wrestling move? To jump up into a lateral position, and fall?

Cena's dropkick, much like Cena's hurricanrana, are moves he rarely performs. For a man his size, they are impressive simply in the attempt. Personally, I like that he uses them in moments of desperation. He performs the dropkick and the hurricanrana in such an awkward way. I'd say he does them badly, but the dropkick he used against Del Rio is the same dropkick he always uses: short, desperate, and half-connecting. John Cena performs these moves as if he learned them in wrestling school, used them for the first couple of years of his career, and then almost never again, because he found better wrestling moves to perform. But sometimes, in a pinch, he returns to an old standby. Instinct kicks in and he's a student again, young and hungry and more willing to hurt himself. And this is *actually* true, which is why I enjoy these moves. Cena's dropkick is informed by his character, and its relative lousiness is caked in consistency. Cena is a great strongman and can absorb a ridiculous amount of punishment, but agility is not a high score on his trading card. Yet there he is, leaping. Or trying to leap.

John Cena attempts few dropkicks, but misses almost none of them (few of his hurricanrana's are countered, as well), and there's a good reason for this: Cena never extends his legs properly for the move, and he would look like an idiot if the dropkick missed. Cena's awkward dropkick requires his opponent to be *kind of* hit by it, but not all the way, because it is an obviously half-charged maneuver. Del Rio recovered from the dropkick rather quickly, as do all Cena's opponents in this position. Cena's dropkick then becomes only part of a whole wrestling move; the second part is the reaction. A wrestling move is performed, and then reacted to.

There's no such thing as a wrestling move performed by one. You'd think that wouldn't be true, especially when it comes to the dropkick. I mean, you can perform a dropkick all alone, right? But you wouldn't be. You'd be performing half the move, a missed dropkick at best, or an imitation of a missed dropkick, since a missed dropkick assumes that the intention was to hit *something*.

Something happens you didn't mean to happen, but knew it had to occur. What difference does it make if someone else is there? Someone you aimed at. Someone you missed. Someone you were supposed to miss. Someone you're paid to miss, have to miss—the whole thing goes tits up if you don't miss. Connecting is not in the script. You fall. You have to fall. They hold on. They escape. You do your job.

You go home, and you wonder if it had hit, if you'd timed things better, where would you be? If you had been in a slightly different place, if your responsibilities had not placed you elsewhere, it would all be different. You would stand taller, move faster, boats against the current and hit, hit, hit, hit, and there wouldn't be outside interference, and there wouldn't be a man paying you to miss, a man you don't like, can barely tolerate, a man who signs contracts. A man you curse in your mirror every morning because he makes you miss. A man you feel powerless to confront, a contract you feel powerless to contend. All you can do, all anyone in this situation can do, is miss well and wait.

BOB BENSON

JULY 8

I sometimes forget that Monday Night Raw is a three-hour show. It is lengthy, and watching from 8 to 11 feels like a hell of a long time. I don't know if it's because I watch other shows piecemeal now, 20 or 40 minutes at a time, but watching Raw live is a marathon. I do not do it every week. I couldn't. Who could watch that much television? When would you get anything done? Do people who watch soap operas watch it every day? Don't they ever take breaks? They have to. They have to take some time off. It's great to have vices—and god knows all these serial fictions are vices—but one has to breathe.

I'm thinking about this because I actually couldn't imagine missing an episode lately. I haven't watched every moment of every episode live but I find myself always catching up lately. WWE has been on a roll since Wrestlemania, and my decision to write reviews since then has been exceptionally rewarding. Before the big night, I actually hadn't watched an episode of the show since January, a near three-month break that was utterly refreshing. I've been consistently watching (and reporting) since the beginning of April, and I actually don't feel tired of it yet. More and more, I'm trying to watch it as it airs, top to bottom, which has not been my MO for years.

That's not just the product of course, but how I'm going about this column. I'm actively trying to get something out of it, and that something isn't necessarily entertainment. I am not writing about Monday Night Raw because it's an exemplar of greatness. I am writing about it because it is messy. It is the messiest show on television, and I need a really messy show right now. I need things that are not perfect. I need things that are sometimes poorly conceived and shoddily thought through. In writing about Raw, I am writing about myself. In trying to find the heart of Raw, I'm slowly clawing through insecurities, complications, catharsis, mistakes, and nightmares. I am watching Monday Night Raw and writing about it because it makes me feel better. It's not as good as therapy, but it is a therapy.

I learn about myself through watching the show. I remark on the feelings that go through me as I watch a lengthy series of moves, interlocking tangos loosely threaded. Listening to the announcers is another thing; I still generally don't like that part of the show. I've become accustomed to largely tuning them out, but they impact the program, and I still generally prefer to watch the show while listening to something else. I'm convinced it's because I want to view the program and decide the meanings for myself. The commentary team is there for the novice. I don't need their explanations or theories.

Watching without the white noise also gives Raw a more autonomous quality: this circus is happening, and it's up to you to discern why. This week, for me, was all about comfort.

I felt a lot of comfort while watching this episode. I was happy to see characters I've kept up with for years continue to shine. Randy Orton hasn't seemed important since early 2011. Last week he fought Christian, who he feuded with that summer, and tonight he fought CM Punk, who he fought in the spring. It reminded me of a time when you could kind of figure out why he existed as a character. This resonated throughout, from Alberto Del Rio's athletic exhibition (they should do their best to make him only wrestle smaller performers) to Mark Henry's effective threat against John Cena. Everyone hit their marks. Everyone played a fairly excellent version of themselves, and lost and won in ways that they should have.

Kane was a phenomenal target. A man who knows a thing or two about cult behaviour was the perfect first victim for the long-hyped Wyatt Family. This new ensemble (well, new to the flagship program) had quite the entrance. A 'reporter' was sent to their backwater house, large and dilapidated, the perfect mix of redneck hoarder and potential murder estate. The reporter was guided by one of Wyatt's disciple's, and through three or four half-minute segments throughout the night, communicated the proper rural creepiness. When he finally appeared, he appeared by lantern-light, walking slowly forward towards us until the camera panned and he sat in his rocking chair while his men took care of business. Those of us who live in cities have long been in contention with our rural family members, who tell us that our metropolis is filled with crime and pollution and heartlessness. And they're right of course, but they fail to mention that the country has people like Bray Wyatt.

But I was also comforted by the messiness, and boy was this episode messy. The backstage skit involving the participants of the Rudos Money in the Bank ladder match next Sunday was laughably horrible, awkward, and a severe reminder that there are no heroes in that story. Ziggler's interference in Del

Rio's match was ugly. And it was difficult to watch just how contorted the Vickie Guerrero performance review became. In a soap, no matter how little one likes the characters, there's a weird and sick and unhealthy comfort that comes from seeing them eat one another alive.

Still, Vickie will be just fine. This is what, her fifth firing? It's like Joey falling down the elevator shaft. Long live General Manager Bob Benson.

Brad Maddox just showed up one day. He was a referee, and nobody seemed to really notice him. Then one night in October, in the middle of a gigantic steel cage, he decided to screw a monster out of a championship title match. His reason? He just wanted to be part of the show. He wanted to be important. Brad Maddox debuted his fashion sense and motive, but we still didn't know anything about him. He fought the monster, and lost irrecoverably. They put his two-dimensional corpse in an ambulance. And then he returned to the wrestling show not to wrestle but needle Vickie Guerrero. Since what, December I guess, he's been on the show every week, very slowly driving Vickie nuts. All we know about him is that he wants to be there. And now he's got her job. Because he's a shit.

"I'm gonna pick up where you left off," he says, grinning like a jackass, before Vickie slaps and claws at him in a final moment of her wonderful character. And in an equally delicious moment, Vince helps Vickie then immediately shakes her off, and grumbles. "You've wrinkled my jacked." Brilliant.

Finally, I was comforted by the production snafu when Christian emerged. On the screen where his name usually shows up, for a few seconds we all saw Michael McGillicutty's wordmark. Why haven't they deleted that file? Why is that still on the hard drive?

I'm comforted by these negative aspects because Raw's imperfections are reflections. Who hasn't hit the wrong button? Who hasn't spent too long in a meeting? Who hasn't told a terrible joke in a room where way, way, way too many people heard it? I'm often bothered by the imperfections I find in other shows, but

Raw's flaws never bother me too much. It's flaws are my flaws. I'd be a hypocrite to attack them.

One last thing. Hug the Vickie Guerrero in your life. Ryback did. It'll make you both feel better.

THE GIRL

JULY 15

So there's this girl. I saw her for a second. I'm generally not the type to take pictures of strangers, so I don't have a photo. I'm going to try to describe her to you. Early twenties. Maybe a couple inches above five feet. A really wide set of perfect teeth, and I know this because when I saw her she was smiling incredibly, like she'd just won a contest and the reward rocked. She's just happy, so happy, her eyes beginning to water behind her makeup.

Beaming with pride. She's got her sign lifted high and she's hopping up and down, hoping to get a glimpse beyond the raised hands in front of her. Her skin was caramel, and the shade made it impossible to call an ethnicity. She could have been literally born anywhere and it would make sense, which is perfect because she's in a sea of people from all over the world, all cheering and booing at the same time in a cacophony. Her hair is dyed blonde, burned straight, and she's really pretty, and her enthusiasm is arresting.

She's in the crowd at Money in the Bank, a show WWE put on July 14. She's there to see John Cena, and I know this because she is wearing one of his t-shirts and is holding a sign that had Cena's logo, and underneath, written in pink, "I love you Cena." It's all I could think about as John Cena arrived, entered the ring, ready for his performance with Mark Henry. It stayed with me until this moment, and it'll stay with me a while longer. If you watch wrestling for a long time, you'll eventually pick someone out from the crowd. They'll move you in some way. Maybe they'll be crying and then you kind of end up crying.

Maybe they're furious, and their scorn helps you buy into the high drama of personal betrayal. WWE cameramen are some of the best in the world. Their job is to search for sharp crystals of emotion that will cut you open and bare them to you raw. They found her and showed her to us, just for a second. It was enough to remind me that I don't love *anything* like she loves John Cena.

I don't own a single piece of wrestling merchandise. I've never taken the time to make a sign. And I've never ever cheered for someone with her gusto. I can't get over wrestling. I obsess about it, and it consumes me. But I don't love it, and I know that not loving it unconditionally is what keeps me from cheering. I'm present, and patient, and on my guard. I can't help but wonder when the other shoe is going to drop, when they're going to take something I have found feeling for and squash it. WWE is in the business of toying with our emotions, but at the end of the day they do want us to be happy. They even want Randy Orton fans to be happy, sometimes. Remember that.

I wish I could lose myself in the show like this girl. I wish I could do that with *anything*. I can't turn my brain off. I can't stop analyzing and ruining jokes and butting in, and I'm awkward and messy with my emotions. This girl, cheering like a lunatic, she did this thing before the camera left her. She calmed for a second, and I think she bit her lip, and looked fondly on the scene, elated and *content*. She wasn't just happy; she was—in that fragment of a second, and on the outside at least—without want. Jesus, am I envious of that. I wish so hard to have John Cena appear and have that be enough.

But instead I'm bothered by the heat, my schedule, my dad, and the feeling of certain textures on my skin, and how that feeling can change given the weather and my mood. I am never, ever as happy as that girl looked, and this doesn't mean I'm not happy. I'm just not equipped with the overdrive of polyphonic glee required to lose oneself in a crowd and love, love, love. And I'm *fine*, which is the crazy thing. It's not like I'm not happy to see John, or Daniel, or AJ, or anyone on the show. But I know that when I see them I'm not seeing a person or a character. I'm seeing a plan and a plot. I'm seeing time knuckle forward to the inevitable end of friendships, to mistakes trying to help a lover, to the sad realization that one may never really win the big one, and finally to true and bloody betrayal, of both the self and the universe, to myself and to others, who believed in me, of whom I believed.

And I know the answer. I've always known, even if it's never really sunk in proper. I want to want less. I want to worry less, and expect less. I want to be happy with what I have and am and can be, and I want to be peaceful and content and utterly elated when my favourite thing appears. I want to be a *fan*, the truest and closest kind. I want to feel what that girl feels, and maybe the best way to get there is to accept that there's no path, no effort, and no trick to it. It is not simply or honestly being simple or honest. It is not something one can attain by trying. You can't climb a ladder and grab what you want simply because you *want* to. You have to eliminate the obstacles first.

I wonder if she enjoyed the whole show. I wonder if I did.

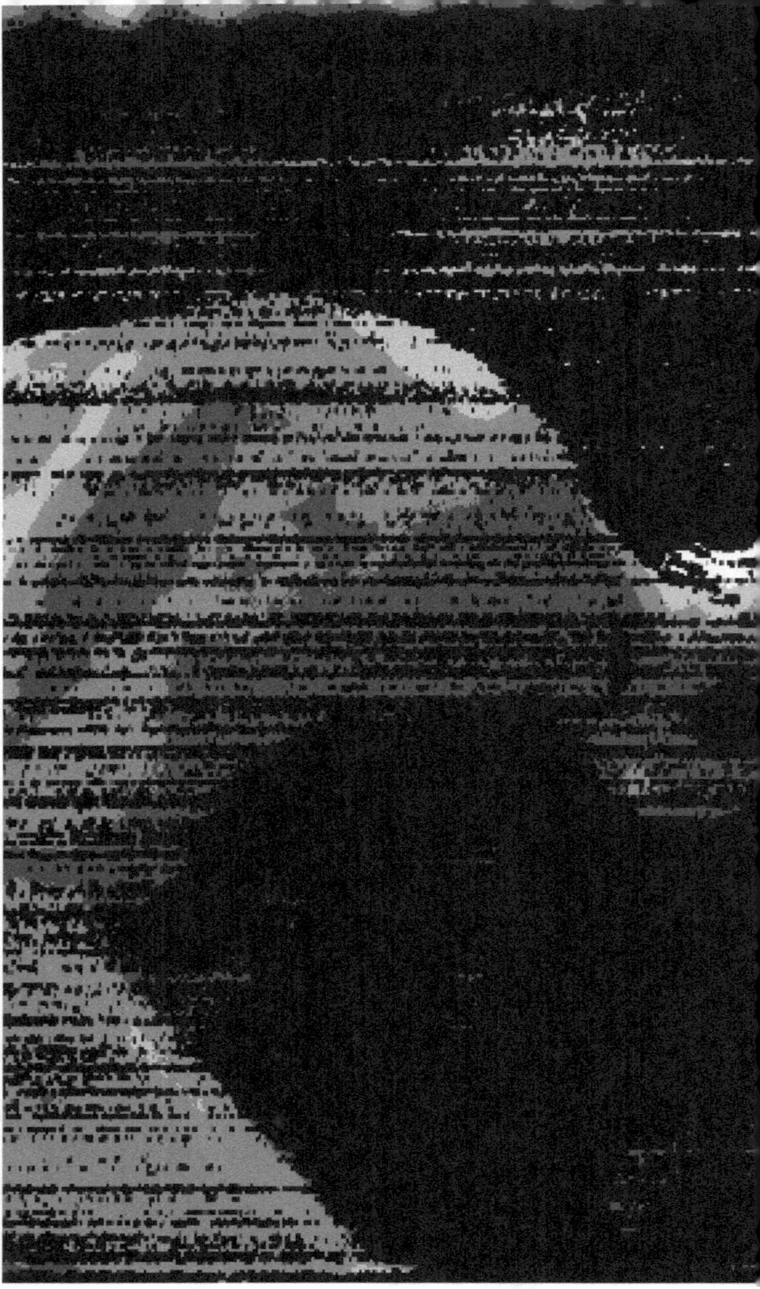

TOTAL DIVAS S1E1

JULY 29

For years, I've wanted WWE to produce a show *about* professional wrestlers that contained little to no professional wrestling. I had a feeling that, if a show were to exist, it would be a huge hit. Pro wrestlers are captivating, energizing people, even when they're completely out of character. They live a unique lifestyle that is perfect for reality television, because their careers dictate constant travel, relatable stress, and a constant barrage of professional and personal strife. These are people who travel from town to town and pretend to fight for a living: the pretend fighting could actually be the least interesting aspect of their lives.

I've also wanted the show to exist because it would inevitably humanize professional wrestlers in a way that's only ever been attempted in documentaries about pro wrestling. Unfortunately, almost every documentary out there is either about the canonical plot of the show proper or something-that-happened-that-was-not-supposed-to-happen. Wrestling docs rarely go further than skin deep on the people involved, and that's something a full series couldn't help but mine. Humanizing pro wrestlers is something I feel could do wonders to not only the show proper (because you would theoretically care about them a little more), but also to the lives of the wrestlers (because the public would see them a little less as a circus act and a touch more like, well, a *celebrity* at least). Even if the show was bad, I'd take it as a net positive.

As a bonus, I'd be even happier if the show promoted the lesser acts of the show, like women, tag teams, and cruiserweights, because those are generally the characters I think need more screen time and are often more interesting anyway. For all these reasons, I have to recommend Total Divas, the new E! reality show about WWE female wrestlers. This week's Raw was taped and not live, and the general atmosphere was that nothing important *should* transpire if a website *could* potentially report it a week early, so almost nothing did. So instead of watching Raw, I watched Total Divas. I'm glad I did. I'll be watching it every single week until it stops, and you should too.

Total Divas is clearly built for the E! audience. The camera work, editing, music, and general tone resemble many of the other reality shows on the network, and the pacing is far more reality than soap. If you like reality TV shows, this is a no-brainer, since you've already accepted the language of that medium and now get to enjoy legitimately entertaining people go through those motions. If you're not (I am in this camp), then it takes a little getting used to. The most important thing I've found with reality TV is that you *can* absolutely skip half the show, because each bumper to and from commercials contains all the exposition you need to follow along. The narrative is spoonfed, and you really can just turn your brain way off.

Total Divas actually bridges the two most popular reality genres—quirky jobs and pseudo-celebrities—and does so with surprising ease. I was delighted that the show was about the work of *being* a pro wrestler in real life, and sidestepped the pro wrestling part almost entirely (because, hey, there's Monday Night Raw for that). This is the stuff that interests me, because we see so little of it otherwise. This show is about the gears at work, the gears one grinds against, and the gears we don't yet understand (like, for instance, just why anyone would think Eva Marie would look good as a blonde).

There are downsides. All the women speak with their outdoor performance voices at all times, which has got to be hell on their vocal chords (it's most noticeable when John Cena is around because, outside of that dinner scene, he's not in performance mode *at all*). The amount of creak in everyone's voices does grate after a while. And the mid-show squabbles come off as just as scripted as, well the kind of squabbles they might actually get in on the show. And I guess that's the thing about going behind the scenes in the wrestling world as opposed to other professions. You are normally hit with a disconnect when you see the curtain pulled back, to see that people are ugly and shallow and self-centered, and you comfort yourself that you're a little more mature and compassionate than the people on TV. But with wrestling, these people are *already* shallow and self-centered and ugly to one another, so it's less of a shock to see them act the same way "in real life." I'm already used to wrestlers acting irrationally.

The episode revolved around Wrestlemania XXIX, and, even for an hour-long show, used a lot of expository catch-up. Every character mentioned how big Wrestlemania was, but it was taken as an assumption that everyone knew what they were talking about. There were also many instances of unexplained actions. Natalya is taken aside and told she won't have a match at the show only a week prior, but wouldn't she have known that already? The Bellas talk about their match without once mentioning the point of it, as do the Funkadacktyls (who were the emotional core of the episode, and are positioned as sympathetic against the Bellas). Finally, when the match at Wrestlemania is cancelled, we are not told why (at least not officially. The Bellas mention that the previous match took too long).

But niggling criticisms aside, this was a tremendous first effort. There have been many attempts in the past to pull back the curtain of pro wrestling, but the lens has always either focused on the negative, or, even worse, revealed nothing. Total Divas has no regard for outdated ideas (Nikki Bella nonchalantly points out that Daniel Bryan's real name is Bryan Danielson; the two tag teams hang out after their match cancellation, both disappointed they didn't get to fight one another). It has no problem pointing out various points of insanity. But it also does so with an overall loving eye. This is a show about the *craziness* of living a pro wrestling life, but suggests that no botched dye job, no angry boyfriend, and no match cancellation can make living it less worth it.

THE KILLING

AUG 6

I want to stress that The Heart is Raw will not always be about Monday Night Raw. Much like International Object is predominantly a wrestling blog but not always so, The Heart is Raw is a pop-cultural emotional essay that just happens to have a lot of Raw reviews. It's just that most weeks, wrestling is the show that moves me the most. But I've always found WWE television to be boring around Summerslam (and I've always found

Summerslam to be the most boring major show of the year. I think <u>Fake Vince</u> had something to say about that). I can't help it: over the past few weeks, my emotional attention has been on The Killing. It reverberates in everything I watch, read, and write. All I can do is worry about what this show is doing to me.

If you're not into The Killing, I completely understand (much like I inherently get why you wouldn't be into wrestling). The Killing is bleak, both in tone and actual colour. The characters are stark and largely unlikeable. The plot is both thin and too complicated, explained through the barest of exposition. Everyone mumbles every line; The Killing is the only show I have to turn up to maximum volume to even decipher (in contrast, I have to turn Raw down). It follows one or two plots for entire seasons, and will absolutely go out of its way to deliver red herrings and false leads. Not everything means something, and there are so few moments of catharsis that the general feeling after the end of an episode is to hate the show.

If you haven't seen The Killing, the basic plot is that of a detective homicide show. There has been a murder, and a pair of cops are sent to investigate. The cops are of different backgrounds (both troubled), and work differently. They have respect for the rules that keep them on their side of the law, but many episodes highlight the tension between seeking justice properly and getting the bad guy. The superior officers in the department are all obstacles to our heroes. There are moments of The Killing that could have been performed on literally any cop show in the last 60 years. But it diverts greatly from there, and the diversions are where it begins to break your heart.

The third season of The Killing has been about finding a serial killer who attracts young teenage prostitutes, kills them, and dumps them in a marsh on the outskirts of Seattle. The setting of The Killing is the extroverted version of the setting of early X-Files episodes: it's always raining, and when it isn't, it's so overcast the entire show is dripped in grayscale (Vancouver and Seattle are pretty similar that way). The sun has shone about 3 times in the last 36 episodes. The detective pair of Sarah Linden and Stephen Holder pair up again after some cast reshuffling. Sarah 'retired' at the end of season 2, but is brought back because the case appears to have something to do with an old case of hers. The man who was put on death row for the old case (Ray Seward, played by Peter Sarsgaard) is about to die, and he's chosen hanging, so that his executioners are forced to "hear" him.

Unlike most cop shows, the case extends through the entire season, which is one of the reasons the show is often so unfulfilling. A cliffhanger on one episode will be explained away as meaningless a few minutes into the next. Some episodes, Linden and Holder actually get nowhere. But the lack of plot propulsion opens up tons of time for character work, and season 3 of The Killing introduces (and concludes) two of the best characters I've had the pleasure of watching all year: Sarsgaard's aforementioned prisoner on death row, and Bullet, a homeless teenage lesbian who becomes Linden and Holder's sidekick.

Bullet (played by Bex Taylor-Klaus) brings a spark to the show that it's never had before. She's never, ever sitting still, and her energy is captivating and desperate. She looks a bit like a 13 year old version of Lisbeth Salander. Her best friend has been kidnapped, and nobody seems to care, so she does everything she can with no money, home, or real hope to get the people with guns to save the day. She doesn't so much transform through the series as emerge, and she inevitably becomes the audience surrogate. Like Bullet, we also want the system to move faster, for people to care more, to believe that our friends are not hurt; we are equally crushed when it does not, when they do not, and when they are have been.

The Killing takes either no pleasure or all the pleasure in removing Bullet from the story. I honestly can't tell. I also can't tell exactly what the writers wanted us to feel in regards to Seward. Through the 12 episodes in which he appears, he oscillates between redeemable victim of the system to psychological monster, and he ping-pongs between the two until you're not sure there is a difference, or that the system has made him this way, or what. Seward isn't innocent, but did he kill his wife? He won't confess entirely or deny it completely, and he takes his own pleasure in confounding the people who actually might be able to help him (specifically, Linden). The last episode in which he appears, The Killing reduces to a bottle episode where Seward and Linden spend most of the time on a prison phone with glass between them. These scenes wrenched me, a near-perfect one act play about justice, time, and how tough it is to actually throw ourselves on the gears. As Seward is given his last words, he quips about his last meal. "Salisbury steak isn't steak. It's ground beef." Justice isn't what it says it is. It's just all we could scrounge up.

Seward's prisoner is the most captivating performance I've seen on TV in a long time. He has such a quiver, and I loved his perverse sense of empathy, his slime, his 0.2 Lector lashings, and how he really did just want to be heard (even if it's just to lie). It was always about volume. He took The Killing's opaque lens, developed through two difficult and frustrating seasons and chewed through it. He broke the show's world. And then it broke him.

The Killing's third season is an exercise in what you can't bear. Linden finds herself unable to bear life without work, and like an addict is most satisfied when being rewarded for her doggedness. Holder, the gruff softie, can't bear himself, can't believe the world is at it is, and he is sometimes equally hard, and when he is there are consequences. Bullet can't bear the thought of being truly alone. Seward can't bear the thought of going down without at least bruising the world on his way out. And the murderer—who I will not spoil—couldn't bear getting away with it. These were all points in which the audience was asked to leave, as if to say: it's only going to get worse from here. It's going to get tougher to bear. The Killing almost dares you to give up on it, and that's why I can't. I don't want to know what that says about me.

You left your keys in the door. I brought you lemon chicken. And fortune cookies. What more could you want?

SUMMERSLAM 1991

AUG 14

WWE has been performing a show called Summerslam since 1988, and every year they've tried to make it different enough from Wrestlemania, while also making it separate enough from all the other shows as to make it seem like a big deal. This has worked some years and not others, but on the whole Summerslam pales in comparison to the biggest show of the year, specifically because it tries to be the second biggest. One can be better, worse, or different, and unfortunately Summerslam often comes across as worse.

Over the last few years, Summerslam has continuously been the least enjoyable major shows of the year. This is attributed to a few things, but my belief is that WWE feels like they *have* to treat it as a big deal, so they do things that don't really make any sense to the canonical product. They'll have feature matches that don't matter the day after they air. They'll have rematches from Wrestlemania that did well and now feel like a rerun. And they'll have strange gimmick matches that don't work *at all*. And sometimes they treat it like a *beginning*, which makes it feel less important than the subsequent fall shows.

I think they do this because they believe some people show up for Summerslam who don't show up for any other wrestling show, and I a) don't think that's possible, and b) don't think Summerslam has ever really been a great 'beginner' show. Plots are generally halfway finished or ending, or don't even really exist. This is how we end up with main event matches like Hulk Hogan vs Shawn Michaels, and John Cena and Daniel Bryan (and some other folks) vs The Nexus. This is how Mick Foley won his last WWE Championship. This is how The Rock ended up with the WCW title.

But this can be great, of course. Not every wrestling show needs to hold up the thread. Not every performance needs to make sense. And sometimes special attractions are worth the trouble. We're always searching for great moments in wrestling, and sometimes they have to come from unexpected places.

For those who remember it, Summerslam 1991 holds a very special place. Top to bottom, the show is insane. I don't mean insane as in awesome: literally none of it made any sense.

The first two matches were spectacular. The six-man tag that opened the show featured three of the most good-guy good guys WWE has ever exhibited. The British Bulldog, Ricky "The Dragon" Steamboat, and Kerry "Texas Tornado" Von Erich strutted out in their most WWE PG outfits and beat up a couple of really, really flat bad guys. It was quick and inoffensive, and was basically the perfect match to start any major show.

Following the brisk (and at the same time, painfully slow) opener was one of the crispest technical wrestling matches in history, and for many years stood as my favourite match of all time. There's not much I can say about Bret Hart vs Mr Perfect that hasn't already been said by countless writers: That it reinvigorated the Intercontinental Championship after years of misuse; that it showed an entire generation of new fans what a great wrestling match could be after years of Warrior/Hogan, and that it 'made' Bret Hart into a star pretty well overnight. I watched it live. Well, I think I watched it live. It was difficult to make out exactly what was happening.

At the time, I was visiting my grandparents. They lived in an apartment that overlooked a small plaza, and in that plaza there was a sports bar. The bar was showing Summerslam on their TVs, and my grandfather and I went down to watch it, only they wouldn't let us in because I wasn't of age, and they wouldn't fudge the rules for even a fan. I was disappointed, and we returned to the apartment. I looked out the window, and noticed that the bar had a patio out back, and I could kind of make out the TV. We were eight floors up, so it was incredibly tiny, but I could definitely see that it was wrestling. My grandfather lent me his binoculars, and I watched as much as I could through them. I didn't make out a whole lot. In fact, I was never terribly sure who was fighting and what happened. But it was at that period in my fandom where I could take literally anything I got, and if that meant only seeing blurry images of maybe wrestlers doing wrestling moves of some manner from eight stories away, that's what I did.

A few months after the event, I acquired a VHS copy, a dub a family member had made and sent me. I watched Summerslam 91 too many times to count. I watched Earthquake and Typhoon get scared from the ring by Andre the Giant (in one of his last appearances). I watched Virgil defeat Ted Dibiase and win the Million Dollar Title. I watched the Road Warriors beat the Nasty Boys in exactly the kind of match you'd think those two teams would have. These were wrestling matches, and I liked them. But I liked the weird stuff a lot more. No other wrestling show I saw as a kid had these kinds of things going for it.

First off, there was a match where the Big Boss Man defeated the Mountie (to prove that American cops were more brutal than regal Canadian horsemen, because this is wrestling and where else are we going to have this debate?). It was fine, but the good stuff happened because of the stipulation: that the loser had to spend the night in jail. Most wrestling stipulations either never feel great in execution (most head shavings), or never happen (all retirings). But this match's stipulation rewarded viewers over several vignettes throughout the evening. The Mountie is arrested, charged, booked, fingerprinted, photographed, and finally stuck in a cell with an overtly gay stereotype (in a scene WWE wouldn't even play today), and this was done with The Mountie ad-libbing comically desperate pleas for mercy.

At one point in the show, Virgil defeated The Million Dollar Man for the Million Dollar Title, a fake title that's way more fake than all the other fake titles in this fake sport. It's so fake that it was purported to cost $125,000 (number pulled from Wikipedia, with the footnote on the number provided by who else but Ted Dibiase himself) a ludicrous number made even more ludicrous that it wasn't even an official championship. Ted Dibiase had it made because he was rich and wanted to show off. And then he *lost* it in a match. To his former *butler*.

You think wrestling doesn't make sense today, that people make decisions that aren't clear. Summerslam 91 has a better analogue to almost anything you'd see today. You think it's zany to have HHH be the referee in the main event? Summerslam 91's main event featured Sid f'n Vicious as the referee. You think wrestler's actions don't always stack up? At one point in the main event, The Ultimate Warrior held up a chair and chased a bad guy off screen, *never to be seen again*. At least not until the next big show, when the legend began that they replaced Warrior with a totally different wrestler.

And to top it all off, this wrestling PPV didn't end with Hulk Hogan posing in victory, as every single one before it had. It ended with Randy Savage getting married to Miss Elizabeth. They tore down the ring and created a wedding scene. Then they played a video, and then these two characters got married. This was somewhat confusing as it wasn't exactly a secret that the two had fairly recently been *divorced in real life*, but that's show business, kids. Oh, Jake the Snake Roberts and The Undertaker spoiled the reception, because of course they did.

Wrestling is silly sometimes. And Summerslam should be when it is silly. It's already the show they market as utterly free of conflict. It's already the 'fun' one. Why not have fun with it? They used to. But it's been a long time.

SUMMERSLAM 2013

AUG 19

Listen. Most of the time it just looks like it hurts. But sometimes it really does.

I sat in a theatre watching Summerslam 2013. Next to me sat an elderly couple. A husband and a wife. They brought their own snacks. They were easily 60 years old. They liked the product. The woman liked the product more audibly. She was there to see John Cena, but she liked Daniel Bryan too. I heard her say he looked like her son. They were visibly angry by what they saw.

Professional wrestling can be confusing. But that's the challenge of the people who make it. Professional wrestling is one of the most opaque art forms around. The job its creators have is to communicate their intent as clearly as possible. That's kind of how art tends to go. They fail if you don't get it on some level, even if that means that confusion becomes a maneuver. And so they need rules. I'm going to talk about this particular show by framing it inside a rather famous set of rules.

These are Kurt Vonnegut's lessons for good short story writing, but they work well in many contexts.

1. Start as close to the end as possible.

Any other year, Kane vs Wyatt in a ring surrounded by real fire would be a climatic end to an epic story. But this is not only their first match, this is Wyatt's debut. He's immediately sucked up any of the leftover grunge/goth/juggalo fanbase that still lurks at wrestling shows, and he does so with such little actual effort. It's like the rocking chair has always been there. Still, he's closer to Raven than the

Undertaker at this point, fragile in all the places a new character has to be.

That the villains stole the hero and took him with them suggests he may be joining them (cultists tend to grow), or he may be disappearing for a while. Kane's been around too long to really need a re-tooling. Maybe the Wyatt's could capture and brainwash R-Truth and Zack Ryder?

2. Every sentence must do one of two things-reveal character or advance the action.

Many complained that Cody Rhodes vs Damien Sandow was too short, and didn't accomplish enough. I believe they communicated everything they needed to in order to move both characters forward exactly one unit. That may be small but it also may not. Cody's measured rise has been 5 years in the making, so baby steps should be expected. Cody showed up to defeat Sandow and he did that. Sandow continues to move forward because he has a macguffin that guarantees a big-ticket item in the near future. Cody moves forward because he's just a little bit better and brighter. What this match accomplished was an ending, a jeweled and rare thing in wrestling. Both characters have now earned the right to tell new stories.

3. Every character should want something, even if it is only a glass of water.

Christian's motivation for fighting Alberto Del Rio for the World Heavyweight Championship was about opportunity, not capitalization. "I just want one more match," isn't actually the same as saying "I'm going to win." Del Rio was light on motivation here, but in general that's the characters problem. He's so obsessed with winning and holding championships he's never really become a person. Christian is exactly the opposite. He's maybe the most relatable character on the show, and few weren't moved when his attempts were not up to snuff, when his own body failed his pursuits. Christian is so human that the villain didn't even need to cheat to beat him.

4. Give the reader at least one character he or she can root for.

The medium is also a reality show, being filmed at the same time with different cameras, to be aired on a different date on a different channel. If it were not for this other show, there would be fewer women in the product. They would have been bumped for time constraints, but politics can sometimes be nice. Natalya is the de facto sympathetic character on Total Divas: the consummate professional constantly looked over for superficial reasons. She hasn't delivered a great performance in a long time and this wasn't one, but it was nice all the same. The villains had great outfits (the only thing befitting the general theme of a Tarantino-esque Los Angeles retro summer), and it was a natural way to get Eva Marie on the show proper.

5. Be a Sadist. No matter how sweet and innocent your leading characters, make awful things happen to them-in order that the reader may see what they are made of.

Brock Lesnar is a tremendous villain. He's too strong and too talented for most wrestlers to even try to fight him. He's intelligent and wrestles with craft and cunning, and he's also insane and not in control of the sounds that come out of his mouth. But he also (and this is most important) *does not care about professional wrestling*. He does it because it is a great living and he was able to convince WWE to give him a large contract for almost no performances, but he clearly does not like doing it. In Chuck Klosterman's new book *I Wear the Black Hat* he defines evil people as those "who know the most and care the least." Paul Heyman is exceptionally smart, but he can't be evil because he cares. We know he cares about wrestling, because he could have left many times and he's still there, playing various roles, including himself in the chaos, and getting punched in the face. Brock Lesnar shows up twice a year to collect a paycheck and destroy a man. If the man somehow luckily defeats him, it*does not matter,* because he has no skin in the game. Beating Brock Lesnar doesn't give anyone anything.

That's why it meant more for Punk to lose. He's lost all year, first to the Rock, then the Undertaker, and now Lesnar. But the outcomes are less important than the fight itself, and this has never been truer than with CM Punk in 2013. CM Punk always told great stories, but his opponents were rarely up to snuff. CM Punk's opponents this year were all guys who are not on the active roster (even Jericho, now that I think about it). These performers only come back when there's something special to do, and this year all four of them came back in part to dance with CM Punk.

6. Use the time of a total stranger in such a way that he or she will not feel the time was wasted.

Big E Langston debuted in January, and he is already being featured on PPVs as a threat. In this case, it was in a mixed tag match that finished a story that's been going since about that time. He teamed with AJ Lee, the current best character in professional wrestling, to fight her ex and her ex-best friend. They figured out long ago that wrestling was a lot more entertaining when they added personal stakes. It made the characters ugly, but also tougher to ignore. Every character in this match was petty. Every character was also must-see.

They were succinct, but they had to be. There are only three hours in which to fill all this content, and the match only really needed to accomplish two things: have Big E lose (finally, a PPV win for Dolph Ziggler in 2013) and have Kaitlyn gore AJ into the earth. They accomplished both in less than ten minutes. But if they had a little bit more time, I feel like all parties involved would have loved to go for broke and have the women fight the men. Kaitlyn is strong enough to tackle Big E. AJ is flexible enough to put Dolph Ziggler in a submission maneuver and choke him out. Sooner or later, this is the group of performers who are going to change perceptions of what a pro wrestler can and cannot do (both in and out of the ring). Let them soar already.

7. Write to please just one person. If you open a window and make love to the world, so to speak, your story will get pneumonia.

Daniel Bryan vs John Cena was an incredibly focused, tightly choreographed match. I don't know how many people noticed this, but they stayed in the ring almost the whole match and were never more than a foot from one another (unless Bryan was running from pillar to post). It was the kind of match William Regal always seemed to want to see, and I can't help but think a guy like Regal was the intended audience. They did not play to the rafters, but the rafters loved it anyway.

John Cena kept up with Bryan and delivered more than what anyone expected of him, and he did so while the entire crowd was telling him he couldn't. He didn't carry the match, but neither did Bryan. They danced together, beat for beat, slap for slap, slam for slam. John Cena and Daniel Bryan gave us one of the most thorough exhibitions of world class pro wrestling I've ever seen. But why did Daniel Bryan win? Because he was better than Cena? That's not why pro wrestling matches go one way or another. No.

Daniel Bryan won because WWE wants you to feel it when they finally stab you in the heart.

8. *Give your readers as much information as possible as soon as possible. To hell with suspense. Readers should have such complete understanding of what is going on, where and why, that they could finish the story themselves, should cockroaches eat the last few pages.*

Viewers of the last month of WWE programming could see Randy Orton appearing, likely cashing in his Money in the Bank briefcase, and robbing Daniel Bryan of his moment. But this did not happen. Randy Orton didn't rob Bryan of *anything*. He *got* his moment. John Cena shook Bryan's hand and raised it and gave him the stage. HHH, the special referee, shook his hand and helped with the "Yes! Yes! Yes!" chants. Confetti and streamers appeared. Fireworks erupted. Rise of the Valkyries rang loud. Cameras panned back, showing the jubilant scene. And because you've seen a few endings like this, you can almost picture the show fading to black. They let you believe in this. But of course you knew better.

Randy Orton did finally appear, but it felt like the beginning of a new show, as if they transported the first scene of Raw to the tail end of Summerslam. He teased cashing in, and then he teased not doing it, and then HHH hurt Daniel Bryan. Orton entered, delivered the briefcase, and pinned Bryan, winning his first WWE Championship since the Miz stole it from him in the cold autumn of 2010 using the exact same method.

They delivered exactly the ending they suggested throughout the story, so it cannot be considered a surprise. Even the villains played by some semblance of the rules. Summerslam saw villains win not by breaking the rules, but bending them to their comfort, skewing the notion of justice just enough. It makes us yearn for something better. It makes us wonder if the damned rules do anyone a bit of good.

But WWE has to explain the rules over and over. They have to explain how they can be broken and bent and manipulated. They have to do this to paint their world, to show us this strange place and how we best traverse its notions of justice.

Because, listen. Most of the time it just looks like it hurts. But sometimes it really does.

ACKNOWLEDGEMENTS

I wrote these articles in the hopes of inspiring and impressing a select group of people. This group includes (but is by no means exclusive to): Richard H Thomas, Jason Mann, Thomas Holzerman, Mitch DeRosier, Razor, Logan Stallings, Scott T Holland, Mikey Llorin, Butch Rosser, Ryan Bayne, Meaghan Hayes, Brandon Stroud, Danielle Matheson, David Kincannon, Ricky Brugal, David Shoemaker, Rachel Davies, Chris Harrington, Robert Dorman,

Joe Drilling, Shelly Deathlock, Eric Allen, Bryan Barrera, Gavin Mevius, Kurtis Dros, Leslie Lee III, Daniella Porcaro, Danielle Stull, Paul Karnatz, Zach Domer, Grace Jung, Bill Bicknell, Virginia Wiglesworth, Colin Young, Trey Irby, Adam Jones, Matt Stoker, Isabella Revilla, Miranda Revilla, and D Louthen. If you think there aren't smart people out there thinking about this art form, pick any name from this list.

That goes for any topic of interest. There is no better way to begin thinking more critically about anything than finding enthusiast writers who can't shut up about it. Follow them, get in contact with them, and help them, if you can. Sometimes they need it.

OTHER WORKS

INTERNATIONALOBJECT.COM

SAWYERPAUL.COM/WORKS

MY LOVER'S PHONE
A RECORD YEAR FOR RAINFALL
NO CHINOOK